# Accidental Bride

*Beaufort Brides, Book Three*

## NOELLE ADAMS

# ONE

Kelly Beaufort stared down at her mostly packed suitcase—lying opened on the bed—and wished she had something sexier to wear.

For her entire life, sexy had never been a word applied to Kelly, either by herself or by anyone else. But still... She was going to Las Vegas for the wild, spontaneous wedding of two of her friends, and she'd liked to wear something appropriate for the occasion.

Only she didn't have anything wild or hot or even particularly nice in her entire wardrobe, which was mostly made up of jeans, tees, and sweatshirts.

"What about this one?" her sister Deanna asked. She was rooting around in Kelly's closet and now stuck out one arm, displaying a rose-colored sheath dress. Both of Kelly's sisters had come over this evening. They'd been planning a sisters' night of movies and chocolate, but after the Vegas wedding was announced, they'd decided to instead help Kelly pack for the trip.

"That's a bridesmaid's dress," Kelly said, straightening her glasses and staring back down at her case.

"I know that." Deanna sounded a little impatient. She was a practical, efficient sort of person, and she didn't like dillydallying about routine tasks like packing for a trip. "You think I don't remember Rose's wedding?"

"You looked beautiful in that dress," Rose added, wiping the dust off the one pair of heels Kelly owned.

"But it looks like a bridesmaid dress." Kelly frowned over at the dress. She'd felt very pretty in it, for a spring

1

wedding in the garden, but it wasn't at all right for a weekend in Vegas.

"It does, kind of," Rose admitted, setting down the shoes and heaving herself up. She was six months pregnant, and so she was curvier than ever beneath her light tunic top. "I wish we had time to go buy you something new."

"I don't need anything new."

"But you never get anything new." Deanna had hung the dress back up and emerged from the closet, evidently having resigned herself to the depleted state of Kelly's wardrobe. "We've spent a fortune on this old house. We should have made sure you had a little money to spend on yourself."

"I don't need a lot of clothes." It was true. It had been true when they'd all been teetering on the edge of poverty because their old-fashioned grandmother wouldn't give up the family's shambles of a historical house in Savannah, Georgia. It was still true, even though both of Kelly's sisters had married wealthy men over the past year and a half.

Kelly didn't do anything but go to classes at a local college and work around this house, helping out her grandmother since she was the only sister who still lived in the old Beaufort house. She had friends, of course, but they weren't the kind that did anything but hang out, watch movies, and eat pizza, so she never needed to dress up. She had a few church dresses and the bridesmaid dress, and otherwise she wore nothing but casual clothes.

Growing up, she'd always been a tomboy, and once she'd gotten old enough, she'd realized it was wiser not to look too pretty or else her grandmother would be trying to marry her off. She wasn't really interested in her appearance anyway, unlike a lot of women. She was twenty-one, but she'd never dated at all. She'd never met a guy who'd made her want to put herself out there. She'd much rather hang out with her best friend, Peter.

Her sisters were the pretty ones. Their grandmother, who had raised them all for most of Kelly's life, had focused all her energy on getting the older girls married off to men who could restore the family fortune. She'd never tried to marry Kelly off, and Kelly understood why.

It wasn't just because she'd made a point of never looking too pretty. It was also because she had no "social graces"—a term her grandmother still used. She wasn't born for marrying a rich man. She was born for staying at home and taking care of the house, taking care of her grandmother.

She'd never minded her position at all. In fact, she'd made sure she was never part of her grandmother's manipulations. But, for the first time, staring at her old buff-colored heels, she wished she were a little bit prettier, a little bit sexier.

A little bit *something*.

Deanna apparently read something on Kelly's face. She ran out the bedroom door saying, "I'll be right back."

Rose shook her head and gave Kelly a little smile. "I wish I could still run like that." She rubbed her hands over her rounded belly.

Deanna was twenty-eight—beautiful, tiny, and curvy. Rose was twenty-six—slightly taller, slightly curvier, and just as pretty. Kelly, at twenty-one, was the tallest of the sisters, and she wasn't curvy at all.

In less than a minute, Deanna returned to the room, holding her purse.

"What are you doing?" Kelly demanded, knowing immediately what her sister was thinking.

Deanna dug into her wallet and pulled out several bills. "Here," she said, thrusting them at Kelly. "When you get to Las Vegas, go buy yourself a really nice outfit."

Kelly backed away, nearly bumping into her dresser. "I don't want your money."

"I don't care if you want it or not. You're going to take it."

"I don't need a new outfit."

"Yes, you do," Rose put in. She was usually soft and rather gentle, but she looked just as stubborn as Deanna at the moment. "You never do anything nice for yourself."

"I do plenty nice. It's your money. I'm not going to just take it. We've taken enough from you and Mitchell as it—"

"You haven't taken anything, and Mitchell wants you to be happy, just like I do." Deanna's little chin was sticking out in a familiar expression that proved she wasn't going to back down. "Take it. Seriously, Kelly. I'll be really upset if you don't. You've always done more than your share for this family. You're always cleaning, or cooking, or hammering down loose boards, or trying to organize all the Beaufort collections—not to mention putting up with Grandmama constantly. I know how hard it must be for you, and you've never complained—"

"I haven't done anything hard—"

"Yes, you have," Rose interrupted. "You're always working. You just turned twenty-one, and you deserve to have a little fun. Do it for us, Kelly. Buy yourself a pretty dress. Do something wild and crazy for once in your life."

Kelly felt incredibly self-conscious. She didn't like to talk about herself, and she didn't like being put on the spot like this. She was used to working around the house, and she loved her grandmother and didn't mind living with her since her sisters had left home. She didn't feel like any sort of a martyr or sacrificial lamb.

It was just life. You did what you needed to do for the people you loved. You didn't need to be paid for it.

The truth was she liked her life. She loved the old Beaufort house, and she could sympathize with her grandmother's desire to keep all of the old family treasures around her. There was something about the familiarity, the history, that was safe, secure—an unchanging haven in a world that often felt out of control.

But she stared down at the bills Deanna was offering. She did want a new dress. She did want to feel different, special—for at least one evening of her life. And she had no money of her own. The family had always insisted that she not work until she finished college since the other sisters hadn't gotten a chance to go to college until recently.

Surely it wouldn't be so bad to accept the money this once. It wasn't like Mitchell and Deanna couldn't afford it. They wouldn't even miss it.

She took a shaky breath, raising her eyes to Deanna. "Mitchell wouldn't min—"

"Of course Mitchell wouldn't mind. This is money I earned from my beadwork anyway. I sold a couple of clutches last week. But, either way, the money is *ours*—not his or mine."

"I can't take—"

"Yes, you can." Evidently getting tired of the argument, Deanna glanced around until she found Kelly's purse on the desk, and she went over to stuff the bills inside. "There is nothing that would make me happier than making sure you have a good time. When you get to the hotel tomorrow, you can find something in one of the shops. Promise me you'll buy something pretty and extravagant."

"Deanna—"

"Promise me."

Kelly sighed, feeling a swell of affection and gratitude, which left her rather shaky since she never considered herself a particularly emotional person. "Okay. I promise."

Deanna smiled, and Rose clapped her hands. "As soon as you buy your outfit, put it on and send us both a picture. I wish we could come with you to see in person."

Kelly couldn't help but grin. "Okay."

"And don't wear those braids," Deanna added. "Your hair is so gorgeous. Wear it loose for once."

After starting to object to this, Kelly decided not to even bother. "Okay."

"And put on a little makeup," Rose said, showing one of her dimples.

"Okay. Anything else?"

Deanna slid Kelly's wallet back into her purse, patting it in satisfaction. "And have a couple of drinks. You're twenty-one now, and you never even went out to celebrate being able to drink legally."

Kelly hadn't. She'd never had an alcoholic beverage in her life, except a few sips of beer that she'd found incredibly unpleasant. She'd just never had the urge to do things like that.

She'd always been hardworking and boring and responsible.

"But don't go too crazy," Rose put in. "Don't get drunk and go off with a stranger or anything. Make sure you're with someone you trust."

"Peter will be there," Kelly said. "I'm sure I'll be staying with him most of the time." When she saw her sisters exchanging looks, Kelly rolled her eyes. "Don't be stupid. Peter and I are just friends."

"Of course you are," Deanna replied with a smile. "That's always what they say."

"But it's true in our case. There's never been even a hint of anything else between us. He goes out with other girls, you know."

"Okay, okay. Don't get all upset about it. You're just friends. I'm sure you'll find another smart, good-looking, funny, sweet guy like Peter one day—who you'll be more than friends with."

Kelly just frowned. She was used to the teasing. She'd been friends with Peter for more than three years now, having met in the first college class she'd taken. They'd both been majoring in Hospitality Management, although he was older and further along in his degree. They'd hit it off immediately, and soon they'd been hanging out most of the time together, but neither one of them was interested in anything romantic.

It didn't matter if no one else in the world believed that men and women could be friends in a completely platonic way. All that mattered was what she and Peter knew to be true. She liked her life as it was. She didn't need anything else.

It had been hard for her when her sisters had left home to get married. She'd tried to be happy for them, but their departure had left huge holes in her world. At least they were still in town though, so she could see them often. It had been a change but not a brutal one.

Kelly was hoping things would settle down now that their romantic lives had been satisfyingly resolved. It wouldn't be the same for her, but it would still be good.

Rose evidently realized Kelly was getting annoyed because she changed the subject. "So you'll get there tomorrow late afternoon, and you'll go to the hotel and then buy your new outfit. When are your friends planning to get married?"

"Since everything is in one night, we're having the bachelor and bachelorette parties first, in the early evening, and then Gus and Veronica will be getting married at nine or ten.

They want to have some honeymoon time afterward, but they have to get back here by Monday morning, so they're just jamming everything into one night."

Deanna chuckled. "All right then. So you'll have to jam in a lifetime of being wild into one night. Do you think you can do it?"

Kelly was going to buy something pretty to wear, and she was even going to have a few drinks. But she had absolutely no intention of doing anything genuinely wild.

But what she said was, "I'll do my best."

~

"I do not understand why you feel the need to make such a silly trip."

Kelly smiled at her grandmother, despite the lofty disapproval in her tone. "Gus and Veronica are good friends. I want to be at their wedding."

"But it's such a foolish way to get married."

"It's not our wedding. It's theirs. They can get married any way they want." Kelly had lived with her grandmother nearly all her life since she'd been very young when her parents had died. She knew how to manage the old woman's eccentricities, and they almost never bothered or upset her the way they sometimes still upset her sisters.

Grandmama was who she was. She wasn't going to change. There was no reason for her to change. Kelly loved her, and there was no one else like her in the world.

"That is no excuse for a foolish wedding. I expect better of you."

Kelly laughed.

"It is no laughing matter," her grandmother said with a frown. She was a tiny woman—eight inches shorter than Kelly—and she always wore old-fashioned black dresses since she was still in mourning for her husband who had died forty years ago. Despite her small size, she had a dignified manner that many people found intimidating. "I expect you back tomorrow evening without delay."

Kelly had never been intimidated by her grandmother. "What else would I do?"

"I do not know. But young ladies are sometimes foolish when they leave home for pagan cities like Las Vegas."

"I'm never foolish."

"There is always a first time, and I do not trust that young man who is always lurking around you."

"Peter?" Kelly's eyes widened. "What's wrong with Peter?"

"He has eyes on you I do not like."

Kelly couldn't help but laugh again. "You've got to be crazy. Peter doesn't have any kind of eyes on me at all."

"I do not trust him. Be sure not to get too close to him this weekend."

"I thought you would have liked the fact that he's a Blake."

The Blakes had a long history in Savannah, going back three centuries. In fact, their history was even longer than the Beauforts, which Grandmama took so much pride in. Unlike the Beauforts, the Blakes still had family money since the family's seafood franchise had grown so quickly in the past forty years.

"The Blakes are a very good family. It is this young man I do not trust."

"Peter's not going to do anything. We're just friends."

"Do not be thinking of him as anything except a friend. You are not the kind of girl who needs a husband."

Ridiculously, Kelly felt a stab of pain at the last comment. She knew it was true. She wasn't particularly interested in getting married—at least, not any time soon. And she'd always made a point of dressing and acting in ways that wouldn't encourage her grandmother to try to marry her off.

But still… it was a little depressing that her marriage-minded grandmother believed no man would really want her.

And what was so wrong with Peter that he wouldn't be a good choice for any woman in the world to marry?

Grandmama was now eyeing her closely. "Do not be getting ideas, young lady."

"I'm not getting any ideas," Kelly replied with a sigh.

"Good. We must accept the lot we have been given. Morris Alfred Theobald III is looking again for a new wife, but I do not think he will be looking in your direction."

Great. Not even the most obnoxious, unattractive, arrogant man she'd ever met would be interested in her.

"I'm just going to see Gus and Veronica's wedding. Nothing is going to happen."

"Excellent. See that it doesn't."

Kelly genuinely liked her life, and she didn't feel any desire for it to change. But she still felt kind of glum as she stood at the parlor window, waiting for Peter to arrive to pick her up for the airport.

She didn't think she needed to change, but it would be nice if people thought it was even a possibility.

~

That afternoon, Kelly walked with Peter into the lobby of a Vegas hotel. Everything was big and loud and flashy and overwhelming, and she moved a little closer to Peter instinctively.

This wasn't her kind of place at all. She didn't like to be surrounded by so many people, and she didn't like the myriad of lights and colors and dazzling displays. It made it hard for her to think. Maybe her grandmother was right. She wasn't cut out for this kind of thing at all.

"I don't understand why so many people come here for vacation," she murmured.

"Where would you go if not here?"

"I don't know. Anywhere. A bed and breakfast on a lake in the mountains sounds pretty nice. This is just so loud and glitzy."

"They do it on purpose," Peter said. "They think, if they dazzle you with overstimulation, you'll spend more money."

Kelly felt better at the sound of his dry voice and the slight arch of one of his eyebrows, a distinctive look that was pure Peter. He had longish light brown hair and steel-gray eyes, and he was dressed casually in worn jeans and a plain gray T-shirt, which she knew could be bought six in a pack from a discount store.

"The only money I have to spend I've already promised to spend on a new outfit for tonight."

Peter evidently found the check-in desk because he steered them to the right. Kelly still couldn't see anything but a lot of motion and shiny objects.

"You're not going to gamble at all?" Peter asked.

"Of course not!" Kelly was outraged by the very thought. After scraping for every penny as she'd grown up, she found the idea of handing over money without knowing exactly what she'd get in return almost offensive, even if it was just for entertainment. "I'm not going to throw my money away. Anyway, Deanna would never forgive me if I didn't spend it on a dress. She gave me a bunch of cash with strict instructions."

They'd made it to the front desk, but they had to wait in line before they checked in. Peter's eyes were resting on her face as he said, "That's good. You never do anything for yourself."

"Don't you start that too. To hear my sisters talk, you'd think I was some sort of noble martyr withering away from her self-sacrifice."

Peter chuckled. "I wouldn't go that far."

She gave him a poke in the side since it sounded like there might have been some irony in his words.

He had a way of talking that always hinted at something else, a deeper intent underlying his words. It was like he invariably meant more than the obvious. She liked that about him, but it sometimes made her nervous since he was often very difficult to read.

Kelly liked to understand people, and she didn't always understand Peter.

"Do I get to help you pick out a new dress?" Peter asked, stepping forward as the check-in line moved.

"Sure, if you want to. I could go with Heidi though. She should be here in another hour or so." Heidi was flying in from California, where she'd been visiting her family, so her plane was arriving later. Kelly hoped she wouldn't have to go shopping with Heidi. She liked her friend, as much as she liked Veronica, the bride-to-be, but Heidi had a taste for in-your-face-sexy clothes that would never work for Kelly.

"I'll go with you. I don't have anything else to do. Owen got here earlier, but he's probably already holed up, playing video games."

"Okay. Sounds good."

Kelly would rather hang out with Peter than almost anyone else in the world, but she suddenly felt a sliver of self-consciousness at the idea of his tagging along while she tried to pick out something sexy to wear.

Peter didn't think of her as sexy. She'd never thought of herself as sexy. She wasn't sure how, between the two of them, they'd be able to find her something appropriate to wear.

~

As Peter had predicted, Owen was already deep into a shoot-em-up video game when Peter made it up to the room they were sharing. Owen was an okay guy, but Peter had little patience with the kind of person who spent every spare minute of his life playing games.

Peter was twenty-four, so he was a little bit older than most of the others he hung out with, all of whom were still in college. When Peter had been eighteen, instead of going to college, he'd taken off to hitchhike his way through Europe, and then he'd kept traveling through Asia and Australia—mostly because he hadn't wanted to go home.

His family was old money, and they had most of the bad habits that came with it. He'd felt smothered by the pressure and all the expectations, and so he'd finally just walked away.

When he'd come back, he'd been determined to earn his own living, so he was working full time so he could pay for college, which was why he still hadn't graduated. He wasn't remotely tempted to go back and live off his family's money, but sometimes he felt like a babysitter, surrounded by people younger than him, with a lot fewer life experiences.

Except for Kelly, of course. Everything was different with Kelly.

Owen glanced away from his game long enough to point toward the bed he'd claimed as his. Then Peter put his bag down and sat on the other bed.

He hated Vegas. It just wasn't his idea of a good time. If Kelly hadn't decided to come, Peter would have found some excuse not to go too. He'd much rather be biking or hiking or traveling somewhere with a history and culture that gave it real depth—or even sitting at home watching TV.

But he was here now, and he knew Kelly was excited about the trip. She'd never really gotten the chance to go anywhere. Sometimes he wanted to shake her grandmother for never giving her a chance to have any fun.

He was thinking about Kelly and how she might look in a new dress tonight when his phone rang.

He almost didn't pick it up when he saw it was his mother, but then guilt caught up to him, so he answered the call after all, moving into the bathroom so he could have some privacy, although Owen seemed completely unaware of his presence.

"Hey, Mom."

"Peter, where are you? Are you out of town?"

"Why do you ask that?" She always seemed to know what he was doing. Occasionally, he suspected that she had spies on him.

"Jess said you weren't at work."

Jess was his younger sister, who came to see him sometimes at the hotel where he worked.

"Yeah, I'm out of town. A friend is getting married in Vegas this weekend, so we came out too."

"Vegas? Well, don't do anything dangerous there." His mother was old-school southern, with the heavy accent and notions of propriety that came with it. "Did your young lady come with you?"

"She's my friend, not my young lady. But, yes, she's here too."

"I don't know why you never take her by to meet us."

Peter managed not to groan. "I have a lot of friends you never meet."

"Of course, dear. But she's special, isn't she?"

He didn't answer, partly because he was embarrassed that his mother had been able to read him so easily and partly because he didn't know what to say. Of course Kelly was special. But no one in the world knew that—particularly not Kelly.

"A mother can tell," his mother added. "I don't understand what young men are thinking these days—sitting around and hoping a lady will just drop into their laps from on high. You have to step up, dear, and pursue her, if you're really interested in her."

"Mom—"

"I know, I know. It's none of my business. I just worry about you, all by yourself out there."

"I'm not all by yourself. You didn't expect me to still be living with you at twenty-four, did you?"

"I don't see why not. You know, Martha Harris's son still lives at home, and he's almost thirty. You'd be so much more comfortable here, or we could buy you a nice place of your own, if you'd just—"

"I don't want to join Dad in business," he gritted out. "I don't want to live on money I didn't earn. Why is that so hard to understand?"

"Well, you don't have to be mean about it."

Peter bit back another groan. "I'm sorry. I just don't know how many times we have to have the same discussion."

"Maybe one day you'll change your mind. I know you want to do hotel management, but your Dad and I could buy—"

"I don't want you to buy me a hotel!"

Occasionally, Peter would wonder if he should just accept his parents' help. He and Kelly had talked for a long time about running a property together—planning out the details of how it would work and what each of them would do. He loved that idea, and he would be thrilled to have it happen more quickly.

But, at eighteen years old, he'd made the resolution that he would earn his success on his own, and nothing in the past six years had changed his mind about it. He'd been steadily saving his money from his job so he could afford a down payment on a modest property when he graduated. It would be a start, and it would be his alone.

"Okay. Okay. I just hate to see you struggling."

"I'm not struggling. I'm working, like most people do. And I haven't finished college yet, anyway. I'll be fine, Mom. I promise I'm not starving."

"Do you have enough money to take your young lady out? You know a woman needs to be wooed if you're going to—"

"I'm not wooing her, Mom!"

Most people would never be in the position to speak those words out loud, but this was his life, and it wasn't likely to change.

She clicked her tongue. "Well, that's your problem, dear. You've got to woo her if you're ever going to win her."

Peter wasn't ready for that yet. He didn't have his degree yet, and he didn't have enough money saved up to really start a life. Plus, Kelly had never once looked at him in any way except as a friend.

Maybe that would change one day, but he wasn't going to ruin what they had if there wasn't any hope for something more.

"I've got to go, Mom. I'll call you later, okay?"

"Okay. Be good, dear."

Peter was shaking his head as he hung up the phone. Surely most guys at his age didn't have their mothers still calling them up and telling them to be good.

He'd already hurt his family enough by his decision not to go into the family business or accept any of the family money. The least he could do was answer his mother's calls.

He and Kelly had agreed to meet in a half hour, and it had only been twenty minutes, but he was bored and restless, so he left the room and knocked on Kelly's room across the hall.

In a few seconds she swung the door open, smiling at him.

His heart gave a familiar little twitch. "I'm early."

"That's okay. There was nothing for me to do in here anyway, except call Grandmama."

"How is she doing?"

"She's fine. Deanna is staying with her for the weekend. Grandmama told me not to let any stray suitors follow me home, so you'll have to keep your eye out for them."

Peter chuckled. If he thought his mother was bad, she was nothing compared to Kelly's grandmother. "I'll do my best to beat them off for you."

"Let me grab my purse, and I'll be ready to go."

Peter watched as Kelly bent over to pick up her purse. Her ass was small and tight and rounded beneath her jeans, and he felt the irresistible urge to touch it. And also her long legs and her breasts and her face and her hair.

But that wasn't likely to happen any time soon.

She came back to him, still smiling warmly—like she liked him, like she wanted to be around him, like she wanted to keep him in her life.

But not like she wanted him in bed with her.

As far as he knew, she'd never thought about him that way even once.

He didn't think he was a bad-looking guy. Girls seemed to like him well enough, even if they didn't know or care that he was "one of *those* Blakes."

He wished a miracle would happen one day and Kelly would see him as more than a friend.

If she gave him even one little sign, he would pursue her exactly as his mother had advised.

But, without at least a sign that she would be receptive, it was too big a risk to take.

~

An hour later, Kelly was staring at a rack of dresses, desperately trying to find one that looked even a little bit like *her.*

18

There was nothing.

All of the dresses were too short, too low cut, too stretchy, too clingy, too sparkly, too wildly colored, or too all-of-those-things-at-once.

She reached for one that was more calmly colored in a solid blue, but then she groaned when she saw it had a diamond-shaped cutout in the front that would display half of her breasts and most of her belly.

Peter laughed and grabbed the dress from her before she could put it back.

"Don't laugh," Kelly said, narrowing her eyes at him. "I didn't see the front."

"You should try it on," he said, his gray eyes still warm and amused. "I'd pay good money to see you in it."

"You shouldn't make fun of me."

"I'm not making fun." Peter's smile faded. "Why would I be making fun?"

She didn't understand why he looked so confused since the reason should be obvious. "Because I can't wear dresses like that."

"Of course you could, if you wanted to. You've got a good body."

She snorted and snatched the dress away from him. There was no reason to feel embarrassed, but she did.

"You do," he insisted, turning to look through another rack of dresses. "You're thin and you've got great legs. You could pull off any of these dresses."

Now she was blushing, which was annoying since she wasn't the sort of girl who blushed. But Peter had never mentioned her legs before—or any other part of her body. She didn't even know he'd recognized that she *had* legs. She kept her face turned away from Peter so he couldn't see her expression. "But they're not my style."

"I know. But I thought your sisters told you to branch out and try something different. What about this one?" He pulled a dress off the rack and showed it to her.

She stared at it, her eyes widening. "I can't wear that."

"Why not?"

The dress was tiny—very short with halter straps and a low neckline. It wasn't as garish as some of the others, but there was a sheen to the pine-green fabric, and she was pretty sure it would fit very tight.

"The color would look good on you. Try it on." He pushed the dress on her, so she had to accept it, and since she didn't see anything that looked better, she went grumbling to the dressing room.

Peter waited outside while she pulled off her jeans and top and stared at the little dress.

What the hell was she thinking? She wasn't the kind of person who could ever wear a dress like this.

"Stop stalling," Peter said from outside the stall. "Just put it on."

"You've gotten really bossy lately," she told him, pulling the dress on and praying it wasn't going to be as bad as she thought. Peter would probably insist on seeing how she looked in it. She wasn't a vain person—at all—but she also didn't want him to think she looked stupid.

"It's just a dress," he said as if he could read her thoughts. "How bad could it be?"

It wasn't bad at all Kelly realized as she zipped up the dress. It fit perfectly, and her bare legs looked very long and slim beneath the high hemline. She even looked like she had pretty good boobs since the neckline accentuated her cleavage.

She stared at herself in surprise, feeling an unexpected swell of pleasure that she was capable of looking so sexy.

"It's good, isn't it?" Peter asked. "Let me see."

"Hold on." At the sound of his voice, she was immediately self-conscious. Was she really going to open the door and show him how she looked in this dress? Was she really going to wear it in public? She wasn't the kind of person who could pull off a dress like this.

What she needed was a sweatshirt to wear over it. Then she'd feel more like herself.

"Open up," Peter demanded. "Let me see."

With a sigh, she opened the door and stepped out, automatically pulling on the straps to hitch up the neckline.

She was too uncomfortable to look at Peter, so she stared at herself in the larger mirror at the end of the dressing room.

Except for the long brown braids she always wore, she looked like someone else.

"Well," she demanded when Peter didn't say anything. "Is it too bad?"

She finally dared to look over at him, and she saw he was staring at her very strangely. Intense. His eyes moved up and down over her body.

She nervously tugged down the hemline.

"It's not bad at all," Peter said at last, his voice slightly hoarse. He raised his eyes to look at her face. "You should get it."

"Are you sure? It's not really me."

"That was the point, wasn't it? Get the dress."

Of course it was. She was supposed to look sexy for once, and she'd found a dress to do that. She must look all right, or Peter wouldn't keep staring at her the way he was.

She pushed aside her embarrassment and nodded. "Okay." She went back into the stall and pulled the dress off. She checked the price one more time to verify she could afford it with the money Deanna had given her, and then she put her clothes back on.

When she and Peter went to pay for the dress, she said, "This feel very strange."

"What does?"

"Buying a dress like that."

"Why is it so strange?"

"Because I've never gotten something like that before."

"Well, you should have. You need to do some more nice things for yourself."

He sounded oddly defensive, which struck her as very sweet. He always looked out for her. Only her sisters had done that before Peter had come into her life. Feeling a swell of affection, she gave Peter a quick, one-armed hug.

He returned the hug with both of his arms, and it lasted longer than she'd expected. But it was nice. He was warm and hard and he smelled really good—like clean laundry and the outdoors. "What was that for?" he murmured.

She pulled away. "That's to thank you for going shopping with me."

"I didn't have anything better to do."

"I know. But I appreciate it. Are you sure I look okay in this?"

"Shit, Kelly," he muttered. "Would you stop asking? You look like a wet dream in that dress. How can you not know that?"

She stared at him, completely shocked by the words, by the idea. He'd sounded grumpy and impatient—not like he was trying to make her feel better—so he must have really meant what he said.

She couldn't believe he'd even had the thought—not in connection to her.

It immediately conjured up a question in her mind about what kind of wet dreams he really had.

But she wasn't used to thinking about Peter in the context of sex, so she pushed the thought from her mind immediately.

"Okay," she murmured, stepping up to put the dress on the counter since the customer before them was finally finished. "I look good in it. We'll go with that."

When she'd put on the dress, she'd felt like a new person. There wasn't anything wrong with the person she'd been all these years, but maybe it would be fun to branch out, try something else.

That was what she was going to do tonight.

After all, what bad could really happen? She'd have Peter with her the whole time, and she trusted him with her life.

Peter wouldn't let her do anything truly stupid.

# TWO

Kelly felt strange and uncomfortable and half-naked as she, Heidi, and Veronica entered a glitzy bar, where they were going to begin their bachelorette celebration.

Both Heidi and Veronica had raved about her appearance—hair loose, new dress, high heels—telling her that she looked gorgeous and she looked nothing like herself.

She should have been pleased by the compliments, but they made it quite clear that she normally didn't look gorgeous at all, which was true but wasn't particularly encouraging.

"You should take your glasses off," Heidi advised, heading toward the bar as if she knew what she was doing.

Kelly followed her friends up to the bar, prepared to order whatever they did since she definitely didn't know her way around mixed drinks. "Why?"

"It would complete the transformation."

For most of her life, Kelly had worn glasses. Even in high school, when all her friends were changing to contacts, she'd kept her glasses. She was used to them. She didn't look like herself without them. "I can't see clearly without them."

"You don't need to see. You need to be seen," Heidi replied with a grin.

"I don't care. I'm not going to go around seeing blurs in the interest of being hotter. This is as hot as I get."

"You look great with your glasses," Veronica said, leaning against the bar and waving the bartender over. "Half the guys here are leering at you as it is."

Surprised, Kelly glanced around the room. While Veronica had been exaggerating, she hadn't entirely been making it up. There were at least a few men who seemed to be staring at her.

She'd never experienced anything like it before, and it gave her the most unexpected flare of pride and pleasure.

When the bartender came over, Kelly ordered the same thing her friends did, a pretty red drink that was sweet and fruity—nothing at all like the sips of beer she'd had before.

She drank several swallows and decided there couldn't be much alcohol in it. She could hardly taste it.

They finished their drinks as Veronica opened the silly little gifts they'd gotten her, and then Heidi decided they should go next door to the "male revue" show. They had another drink there, and by that time Kelly was feeling more relaxed, so she didn't even mind the rather tacky performance of men ripping off their pants and humping audience members.

She laughed and cheered with the others as one of the dancers came over to Veronica, who was wearing a bride-to-be sash, and did his thing with her. At some point one of the others must have ordered her another drink. It was still tasting good, and Kelly didn't feel like she was going to be sick or pass out or anything, so she happily drank it.

As they were leaving the male revue, all three of them were laughing hysterically. Kelly had had plenty of good times before, but she had never felt like this in her life—completely free, as if all of her normal little worries didn't mean a thing.

They were to meet up with the guys in the lobby of the hotel before they all headed for the wedding chapel. When Kelly saw Peter standing with the others, looking relaxed and incredibly cute with slightly mussed hair, a gray suit, and loosened tie, she felt the strangest surge of ownership.

Peter was her friend. And he was the cutest guy around—not to mention the smartest and sweetest and funniest and overall best. He smiled when he saw her approaching, his eyes running up and down over her body.

He liked how she looked. He'd never liked how she looked before.

She was flushed and strangely giddy as she made a beeline toward him, wanting to touch him, feel him, be close to him in a way she never had before.

She didn't know why exactly she wasn't stopping herself since it wasn't something she did, but she wrapped her arms around his neck when she reached him, pressing her body against his. "Hello," she said.

Peter smelled like something strong, biting—whatever he'd been drinking. She didn't know enough about alcohol to recognize it. "Hello," he said, a smile in his voice. "Are you having a good time?"

She *was* having a good time. She was having the best time she'd ever had in her life. "Oh yeah. We watched mostly naked men dance."

Peter frowned. His arms were resting around her waist. "And you enjoyed it?"

In a weird little flicker of her mind, she realized that she normally wouldn't act like this. And for some strange reason, she didn't want Peter to recognize the difference. "It was okay," she said, releasing his neck. "They all looked kind of fake, but it was funny to watch all the girls screaming."

This was evidently close enough to her normal behavior to satisfy Peter. He gave her his adorable little eyebrow arch. "I bet it was. So you didn't do any screaming?"

She had. If truth be told, she had. "I'm not the screaming type."

His eyes were focused on her face, with an expression somewhere between appreciation and questioning.

She liked the appreciation better, so she smiled at him.

His eyes warmed in a way she could recognize very clearly. She liked that.

She really liked that.

"How much did you have to drink?" he asked.

"Not much," she lied. "I didn't even finish the one I had. I didn't want to be sick for the wedding."

Kelly had no idea why she'd lied. She'd never lied to Peter before. She almost never lied to anyone. It just didn't normally occur to her as something to be done.

But the warm, happy fog in her mind was telling her that she would have a much better time if Peter didn't know how much she'd drunk. He always tried to take care of her. He would try to stop her from doing all the things she wanted to do tonight.

And she wanted to do a lot of things—things she'd never done before, things she'd always held herself back from.

Despite her lack of practice, she must be a pretty good liar, because Peter believed her.

His smile widened. "Good. You'll have a better time if you're not totally out of it."

"I'm not out of it at all, and I want to have a good time."

"Then that's what you'll have." He was looking at her that way again, that warm way that also seemed hotter than usual, like he couldn't get enough of looking at her.

It made her feel incredibly gorgeous, sexy, but also a little worried. She patted her hair, which was hanging loose in a way she never wore it. "I need to brush my hair."

"No, you don't," he said, glancing over at the others, who'd been having their own conversations. "We need to get going soon."

"But I don't want to have messy hair for the wedding." She tried to smooth down the length of it—it was straight and fine and almost reached her waist.

Peter's face softened as he reached over to gently touch her hair. "I like it this way."

"Okay. I'll keep it like this then," she whispered, wondering why she'd never seen him looking at her this way before. Maybe she should have made herself pretty and sexy before so Peter would have been looking at her this way the whole time.

She liked it. A lot. She didn't want him to go back to looking at her like a friend.

She wanted him to always look at her in that particular way—like he wanted her, like she was everything to him, like he adored her.

Kelly had never been adored before, and she didn't want it to stop.

She took his arm as they made their way out of the hotel lobby.

She had no idea why everything was so different tonight, just because she'd put on a new dress. But Peter was hers, and she was going to keep him that way.

∼

A couple of hours later, Peter was feeling like all of his dreams were finally coming true.

For the first time since he'd met her, Kelly seemed to want him—in a way that was a lot more than friendly.

He knew she'd had a couple of drinks. She'd had one before they'd met up, and she'd had a glass of champagne at Gus and Veronica's wedding. And then they'd all gotten more champagne afterward to celebrate, but she'd been looking a little flushed, so he'd ordered her water instead. She took a few sips from his glass, but it couldn't have added up to very much.

She was a little tipsy. That much was clear. Her inhibitions were down some, and she probably felt a little buzzed.

But she hadn't had enough to drink to really not know what she was doing.

And she was all over him, like she couldn't stop touching him.

He'd had several drinks himself, and he couldn't stop touching her.

At the moment, they were all in a rounded booth, eating wedding cake and drinking champagne and laughing uproariously at a joke he couldn't even remember.

Owen was responsible for filling up glasses, so he topped them off whenever they got down even a little. Heidi had obviously drunk too much. She was singing to herself rather woozily. They'd have to make sure she got back to her room okay when they left. Gus and Veronica were making out in a way that really should have been kept to the bedroom.

And Kelly…

Kelly was leaning against him, smiling up at him sleepily. Her cleavage was on full display. Normally, he would have tried to be the gentleman his mother had raised him as, but tonight he couldn't not stare down at her low neckline.

She had gorgeous breasts—firm and curved in a deliciously subtle way. He wanted to see more of them. He wanted to see all of her.

"Peter," she murmured, as if she didn't want anyone else to hear.

No one else was paying attention to them anyway.

"Yes, baby." His voice was very hoarse. A little warning in the back of his mind told him that he'd drunk too much to make really good decisions in this, but the rest of him was roaring with desire, with affection, with such deep need.

She rubbed one hand in circles on his chest. "Why have you never come on to me?"

His breath hitched, his heartbeat accelerating until it might pound its way out of his chest. His face was hot. The whole world was hot. "I didn't think you'd want me to."

She blinked up at him, her green eyes wide and deep and trusting. "Did you want to?"

One of his hands was lifting, quite without volition, and cupping her cheek. "Of course I wanted to. How could I not want you?"

She was breathing in choppy little pants. "Even when I'm not pretty and sexy like this?"

"You're always pretty. You're always sexy. I always wanted you."

He couldn't believe he was saying it. Very faint alarm bells were sounding off, but he silenced them by lifting his other hand so he could take her face in both of his hands.

"Are you going to kiss me?" she asked, her hand fisting in his jacket lapel.

"If you want me to."

"I do want you to." Her free arm lifted to wrap around his neck.

Her whole body was draped over his, and he was suddenly aware that he was fully aroused. No wonder he was so hot. No wonder he wasn't thinking as clearly as he should be. A deep throbbing was centered in his groin and surging out to the rest of his body.

With a muffled groan, he tilted his head down to kiss her. She responded eagerly, a little clumsily, opening her lips and sliding her tongue against his.

The arousal deepened until he was afraid he was going to completely lose it, right here in the booth.

He forced himself to lean his head back, parting their lips. His mouth was so dry that he lifted his glass and swallowed down the last half of his champagne. He had no idea how many glasses he'd had tonight—not to mention the whiskey he'd had with the guys earlier.

He needed to stop drinking. Right now.

Kelly didn't fight the end of the kiss. She just leaned her head on his shoulder. "I want to be with you forever, Peter," she sighed.

His heart was about to explode right out of his body. He'd never experienced anything like it before. "Me too. I want that too."

"Good." She was smiling as she lifted a hand to stroke his face. He had a slight five o'clock shadow, and her palm scratched deliciously against it. "But what if, tomorrow morning, you change your mind about wanting to be with me."

"I'm never going to change my mind. I've wanted you for a really long time, baby, and that's never going to change."

He couldn't believe he was saying this. Something wasn't quite right about it. But he couldn't help himself, and he loved how her expression became awed as she heard the words. "Really?"

"Of course, Kelly." He couldn't stop himself from leaning down to kiss her again, very gently. "What can I do to prove it to you? I'll do anything you want."

She straightened up and twisted her body so she could rub against him like a cat. She was smiling in a pleased way, as if she had a little secret.

He loved the expression. He loved all of her expressions. He wanted her to always be happy, always be everything she wanted.

She leaned forward until her mouth was less than an inch from his ear, and she whispered, "I'm going to tell you what I want."

~

Less than two hours later, Peter and Kelly were stumbling into a hotel room together, unable to pull out of a hot embrace.

Peter had gotten them another room in the hotel. This one was very expensive, decorated in crisp white and red velvet, with a huge lush bed in a prominent position.

Peter was hard again. It felt like he'd been hard for the past three hours, although he knew that couldn't be true. But he was all fired up now—hot and fuzzy and thrilled and disoriented and desperately eager to claim Kelly at last.

They were clawing at each other's clothes, and they stumbled toward the bed. Kelly was even more disoriented than he was, so he took off his suit jacket, belt, shoes, and socks before he grabbed her and pulled her into bed with him.

"Peter," Kelly gasped, raising herself up on her knees. She was deeply flushed, her hair a tousled mess, and she still had that sweet, groggy look in her eyes. "Help me with my dress."

He groaned as he found the zipper and pulled it down, watching as the fabric slid down her body.

She was long and slim and perfect, her breasts high and firm, her rosy nipples beautifully tight. She had on a little pair of underwear, so he slid those off too.

He groaned helplessly at the sight of her naked body. His whole body was throbbing in a dangerous way.

"Do you like it?" she asked, looking down at herself.

"Oh, God, yeah." He pulled her back down so she was lying on her back, completely naked now, laid out for his gaze, for his touch.

"I want to see you naked too," she murmured, fumbling clumsily at the buttons of his shirt.

He couldn't wait for her to get it off. He pulled off his clothes in a hot rush and then pulled her into his arms.

"I like this," she whispered, almost shyly, her hands sliding down to take his erection in his hands. "I like being with you like this."

He moaned as she stroked him. "I do too."

Her eyes seemed to be closing. She was licking her lips. Her hair was all over her face. She was the sexiest thing he'd ever seen in his life. And she was touching him. Caressing him. Exactly the way he'd always wanted.

Before he knew what was happening, he felt a wave of pleasure tightening in his body. Tightening so fast and so hard that there was no way he could stop it.

Her hands were all over him, running up and down the length of him, slipping even lower to rub his balls. Tightening. Squeezing. Turning the whole world into a rush of heated pleasure.

"Oh fuck," he burst out, just as climax hit him without warning. His body shook as he released himself in her hands, against her belly.

"Oh, fuck, oh, fuck," he muttered, as his body relaxed, the pleasure followed by a blurred wave of uncomfortable awareness. "I'm sorry."

"What for?" she asked with a smile, still stroking him, staring down at him in pleasure, as if she couldn't believe she'd brought him to climax. "It was wonderful."

She stretched up to kiss his chest, and then she reached down to grab his left hand, bringing it up so she could kiss it too, just over the simple gold band he wore.

She'd bought it earlier from a shop attached to the wedding chapel, using the leftover money she'd gotten from her sister.

He hadn't needed to buy a ring for her. He'd given her the signet ring with the Blake family crest he'd always worn.

It was on the ring finger of her left hand now, a little loose, but he could fix that later.

She was wearing his ring. She was his wife now. That was all that mattered.

She nestled against him, looking not remotely disappointed that they hadn't even managed to have sex.

"I guess I had too much to drink," he muttered, wrapping an arm around her, pulling her tightly against him.

"That's okay." She looked like she was about to fall asleep. Her eyelids couldn't stay opened. "I'm very happy with my husband."

He hoped it was true. He would make sure it remained true, no matter what he had to do to keep her happy.

It was like a miracle had occurred, and the world had turned itself around, finally giving him what he wanted.

The past few hours felt like a blur now. He couldn't even remember all the details.

But the details didn't matter. He had Kelly exactly where he'd always wanted her. Naked in his bed. Wearing his ring. Sweet and affectionate and uninhibited.

She was his. And she'd still be his tomorrow.

He had a marriage certificate to prove it.

# THREE

Kelly woke up in a thick fog.

Her mind was so dark, confused, and cloudy that she could barely get her eyes opened. Her head ached, her mouth was parched, and every part of her body hurt.

After a few minutes, she managed to open her eyes and stare up at a small chandelier.

She'd never seen that chandelier before. It wasn't in her room. It wasn't in any room she'd ever been aware of. She had no idea why she'd been sleeping beneath it.

The idea released a trigger of anxiety. She sat up in bed, groaning as her head ached even more. She was in some sort of fancy hotel room, but she couldn't remember entering this room. When the covers slipped down, she gasped out loud when she realized she wasn't wearing a shirt.

A quick check under the covers confirmed that she was completely naked. Not even her underwear.

She never slept naked. She'd never even dreamed of sleeping naked.

And yet here she was in a strange hotel room, in bed without any clothes, with absolutely no idea how she'd gotten here.

The likely scenario hit her so hard that her stomach heaved slightly. She jerked, ready to run to the bathroom, but the nausea settled into a sick, churning tightness in her gut.

This couldn't have happened.

She was in Las Vegas, she suddenly remembered, for Gus and Veronica's wedding. The bachelorette party came back to her. Drinking those red, fruity drinks. Watching the mostly naked men dance. Deciding to be a little wild for the first time in her life.

She tried to push through the dark fog in her head, and she had a few scattered recollections of meeting up with the guys. She'd been at the wedding. She was almost sure of it. And Peter had been there. She could recall images of his face in passing snatches.

He wouldn't have left her alone. She was certain of it. He would never have let some random man take advantage of her.

She scoured the room for some sign or hint of what she was doing here, and she saw her dress and underwear littering the floor. It caused another heave of her stomach.

There were men's clothes too. A gray jacket from a suit—like Peter had been wearing. A white dress shirt. And a watch on the nightstand. An expensive gold watch with a thick band.

She grabbed for the watch.

It was Peter's, she realized in an intense rush of relief as she checked the inscription on the back. His father had given it to him when he'd graduated from high school. Peter was the man who had been with her in this room.

If it was Peter, then nothing bad would have happened.

She had no idea why she was naked, but it couldn't be any sort of nightmare scenario, not if Peter had been with her.

He'd never let her be hurt. He'd never let her be too stupid.

There was something large and loose on her finger, so she twirled it unconsciously, trying to make her mind work the way it was supposed to.

On that thought, the door to the hotel room opened, and she grabbed for the covers to pull them back up to her shoulders.

Peter walked in, wearing his gray trousers from last night and a white T-shirt. He held two large cups of coffee.

He smiled at her when he saw she was awake and sitting up in the bed. His smile was strangely sweet, almost tentative. "Good morning." He looked so adorably self-conscious she couldn't help but smile back.

"Hi." She reached for the coffee as he approached and had to catch the covers with one of her hands as they started to slide down again.

He sat down on the edge of the bed beside her, his eyes searching her face in an unusually intense way. "How do you feel?"

She took a long sip of coffee, the heat and strong flavor hitting her with an immediate sensation of pleasure.

No clarity though. She still couldn't pierce the dark cloud in her mind.

"Not too good," she replied at last. "My head is killing me."

"We had a lot to drink last night."

She suddenly saw an image of herself, lying to Peter about how much she'd drunk with the other girls before they'd met up with the guys. Of course she'd had a lot to drink.

She'd had *way* too much to drink. No wonder last night was a blur.

She cleared her throat and took another sip of coffee. "What happ—how did I get here?"

Peter's gray eyes had been soft as they rested on her face, but now his gaze, his whole body stiffened slightly. "You don't remember?"

She shook her head. "I don't remember anything. I'm sorry. I remember hanging out with Veronica and Heidi, and then I vaguely remember Gus and Heidi getting married. But I can't remember anything else. Why am I in this room? Why am I naked? I didn't do..." Her breath hitched in another flare of fear. "I didn't do anything stupid, did I?"

Very slowly, Peter reached over to set his coffee on the nightstand. "You don't remember what happened last night?"

"No. I just told you. I did something stupid and embarrassing, didn't I?" She cringed, thinking about the possibilities. Maybe she'd stripped naked in a bar. Maybe she'd been making moves on random men.

Maybe she'd come on to Peter.

That thought was the worst. Surely she wouldn't have done something so wrong, so crazy.

"You only had a few drinks," he said, a strange texture to his voice. It sounded tense. Too tense for everything to be all right. "I tried to keep count so you wouldn't overdo it. You were... buzzed, but you weren't completely wasted."

She glanced away, letting her loose, messy hair hide her face. "I had at least three with the other girls. I don't remember how many I had afterward. I've never really drank before."

He gasped. "You said you only had one."

"I know." She couldn't meet his eyes. She couldn't remember ever feeling so mortified. She'd always been responsible. A very unsilly person. She wasn't someone who ever did anything like this. "I... I didn't tell you the truth."

"Why not?" He was sounding more and more upset.

"I don't know. I'm sorry. I don't know. But I obviously had way too much to drink. Please tell me what I did. It wasn't too... too bad, was it?"

Peter didn't answer.

He didn't answer for so long that she finally peeked out at him from behind her hair. He was staring down at the floor, something tight and conflicted frozen on his face. She couldn't tell exactly what emotions he was feeling, but he was obviously upset.

She was getting so scared that her breath came out in fast, thick pants. She hid behind her hair again, wondering if she even wanted to hear what she'd done in her drunken stupor last night.

How could she have been so incredibly stupid? She'd always been a good girl—so good she was probably boring. Deanna and Rose had always gotten around more than she had, but they had never done anything like this.

Only her. Stupid, stupid Kelly.

"Kelly," Peter said, whatever had been freezing him the minute before dispelling. He reached out to push her hair back from her face and tilt her head up so he could see her. "You're saying you didn't want to... want to..." He had his face under control now, but something deep was going on in his eyes, something that made everything worse.

"Want to what?" Her voice cracked. "Did I... did I come on to you, or something? Did we... spend the night together?"

Of course they had. Why else would she be naked in bed right now, when Peter had obviously slept in the room too? She felt a hot rush of embarrassment.

And a hot rush of something else. Something foolish. Something she definitely shouldn't be feeling about Peter. Not after what had evidently happened last night.

"No!" He shifted on the bed. "Well, yes, but nothing happened. I mean, something happened, but it didn't get very far."

She'd never heard him sound so stilted, so babbly.

"So we didn't have sex?"

He shook his head as he met her eyes. "We started, but it ended before it got anywhere. We were both… totally out of it."

She let out a loud exhale. It didn't sound too bad. It could have been much, much worse. "You were drunk too." It wasn't a question. She knew it was true. Peter would never have let them get into that situation if he had been thinking clearly.

"Yeah." He was staring back down at the floor now, his shoulders very tense. "Not as drunk as you. I mean, I can remember last night. And I thought I… I knew what I was doing. But I obviously didn't. If I hadn't had too much to drink, I never would have believed…"

"Believed what?"

He shook his head. "I never would have let us get into this situation."

"Well, it doesn't sound too bad." Kelly smiled at him, trying to cheer him up. Her head still pounded like a jackhammer, but it didn't sound like anything catastrophic had occurred. "So we were drunk and stupid for a night. At least nothing serious happened."

Peter cleared his throat. "There's more."

"You said we didn't have sex."

"We didn't, but that's not the only thing that happened last night."

He took a strange, shaky breath, and then he placed his left hand on her covers, the weight of it pulling them down slightly from where she'd tugged them up over her shoulders.

She stared down at his hand since she was obviously supposed to. And she blinked several times as she realized that he was wearing a simple gold band.

On his ring finger. Of his *left* hand.

She made a little noise in her throat as she remembered she'd been playing with something on her own finger all morning without even recognizing it. She pulled her left hand out from under the covers and saw that she was wearing Peter's signet ring.

Thick, heavy gold with the Blake family crest engraved on the flat surface.

"What..." she breathed.

"Yeah."

"We got..."

"Married."

"Why?"

"I... I have no idea."

He wasn't meeting her eyes, and she suddenly realized why. This was her fault. It must have been her idea. In her drunken state, she must have come up with this ridiculous notion, and Peter had been in no fit state to refuse.

He'd always been a gentleman. He would never blame it on her.

But it was obviously her own, stupid fault.

"Okay," she said on another taken breath. "Okay. I'm sorry for getting us into this situation."

"It's not your—"

"It doesn't matter whose fault it is, but it's still not the end of the world. We can just... get it annulled or get divorced or something. We'll pretend it never happened. No one has to know."

Peter was still staring at the floor. "Right." He swallowed so hard she could see it in his throat.

With a wave of concern, she reached out to put a hand on his shoulder. "Are you mad at me?"

He inhaled sharply and turned to look at her. "Of course not. I'm mad at myself."

"It wasn't your fault, Peter. I don't care what you tell me. I know I must have been the one to get us into this situation."

"You didn't—"

"Don't bother trying to argue. It's really okay, Peter. I'm embarrassed, but I'm not upset, and I'm definitely not upset with you. Let's get dressed, and then we can figure out how to take care of this. I'm sure we're not the only people who have gone to Vegas and accidentally ended up married."

"Accidentally. Right."

"Right?" He was still acting strange, and she had no idea why. It bothered her—even more than the knowledge of what she'd done when she was drunk.

"Right." He gave her a little smile. "I'll go take a shower if you want to finish your coffee."

"Okay. Sounds good."

She watched him walk into the bathroom. He moved naturally, and he smiled at her again before he shut the door, but she could tell that something was still wrong.

She flopped back against the pillows, taking several more swallows of coffee. She told herself to be practical and reasonable about this, the way she was about everything else.

Her leg moved against something that felt strange on the sheet, so she slid a hand down to check it out instinctively. Her eyes widened dramatically as she realized what it must be.

Dried semen.

"Oh God," she groaned, starting to cover herself up with the sheet but then pushing it down abruptly. She sat up, swinging her legs over the side of the bed. Glancing down, she saw something dried on her bare stomach.

That must have been from Peter too.

She had absolutely no memory of anything that had happened in this bed last night, but evidently it had ended with Peter coming.

Her whole body flushed hot at the realization.

She wasn't supposed to be thinking about Peter like that. He was her friend, and that was what he'd always, only been. He wasn't interested in her in any other way.

They'd been drunk. Men would go to bed with almost anyone when they were drunk. He still wasn't interested in her. He'd been really upset about their getting married.

She stared down at the ring on her finger. This morning she was evidently a Blake. Her grandmother would be so pleased.

If truth be told, it wasn't as horrifying a thought as it should have been.

But none of that mattered. Peter was obviously upset. The only kind thing she could do for him was help him get out of the situation as quickly as possible.

That was what she was going to do. Whatever Peter wanted, she would go along with it. This was her fault, and she wasn't going to let him suffer because of it.

~

Peter stepped into the shower, the water on so hot it almost scalded him.

He hadn't spent his entire life being smart. It was only in the past few years that he'd tried to grow up and do something purposeful with his life.

But nothing he'd done in the past had been nearly as foolish as this.

He'd actually believed Kelly wanted him, wanted to be married to him. He'd let himself believe her inhibitions were down enough for her to act on what she really wanted.

He hadn't wanted to know the truth of it—that she was too far gone to make a good decision, or make any decision at all.

He'd obviously been too drunk too, but he couldn't take any comfort from that excuse.

It had been his mistake. And he would have to live with the way his heart felt broken right now, like he'd lost what he'd almost had.

He stayed in the shower a long time, too wracked with the harsh reality to think clearly or come up with a plan. He only turned off the water when his skin was really starting to hurt.

As he was drying off, he heard a beep on his phone from the pocket of his trousers. He leaned over to pick it up and blinked in surprise when he saw there was a voice message from his mother.

He clicked on it, glad of the distraction. His issues with his parents were nothing compared to the pain of losing Kelly, after thinking for one night that he'd had her.

The message began abruptly.

*Peter, what is this about you getting married? I just got a call from Verna Wilson, who heard it from her daughter, Heidi, who I guess is with you there. She said you got married to that Beaufort girl. Why didn't you tell me? Your dad and I would have put on a beautiful wedding for you. You know we would want to be there. I'm so happy that you decided to be a man about it, but I don't know why you had to do it in such a rush. There are traditions, you know. Anyway, I want to hear all about it, so call me back as soon as you can. Since Verna knows, you can bet all of Savannah knows by now. I can just imagine what old Mrs.*

*Beaufort is thinking. Her granddaughter married a Blake! Call me, Peter. Call me as soon as you can.*

Peter's heart was racing as he heard the end of the message. This was a nightmare. Not only had he been an utter fool, but everyone he knew would find out about it. His mother had sounded so happy beneath her outrage at being left out.

He would have to disappoint her on top of everything else.

He sat down on the side of the tub, his towel wrapped around his waist. He stared down at his phone. His body was buffeted with waves of mortification and loss and grief and self-directed anger.

If he hadn't wanted it so much, he would have stopped this thing from happening last night. He'd known better.

Deep inside, he'd known it was too good to be true, too easy, too much like a fantasy come to life.

Kelly didn't want him. Not like that.

She never had.

A tap on the bathroom door surprised him. "Peter?"

He raised his head at the sound of Kelly's muffled voice through the door. "Yeah."

"Are you okay?"

"Yeah."

"It feels like you're upset in there."

"I'm not upset."

"It feels like you are."

"How can you tell what I'm thinking through the door?"

"I don't know. It just feels like you are. And you've been in there a long time. Can I come in?"

"Yeah."

She opened the door, wearing one of the hotel bathrobes. Her hair was still loose, and it was long and messy and beautiful, hanging down around her body. She'd put her glasses on, so she looked more Kelly-like.

Peter had never seen anything or anyone that he'd wanted more.

Kelly came over to sit beside him on the edge of the tub. "I'm sorry about this," she murmured.

"You don't have anything to be sorry about. I'm the one who got us into this situation."

"How did *you* get us into it? I was the one who was most wasted. It was my idea. Wasn't it?"

He nodded, relieved at least that this was the truth. "But I should have stopped us. I shouldn't have... I should have stopped us."

"But you were drunk too."

"Even so, if I'd been smarter, I would have known that you didn't really want this."

Her shoulders straightened, and she turned to frown at his face. "But you didn't want it either, did you?"

He stared at her, his mouth slightly parted. Of course he'd wanted it. He'd never wanted anything more. But how the hell could he tell her that now when she looked so astonished and upset by the very idea? "Of course not," he said gruffly, looking back down at his phone. "I'd had too much to drink."

Her face and body relaxed. "We both had. It's no big deal. We might have grounds for annulment. We should look into that right away."

He didn't want to have their marriage annulled, but he had no choice in the matter. "Right."

She must have read something on his face because she reached out and put a hand on his thigh, over the towel. "That's what you want, isn't it?"

Maybe he should just admit the truth. Maybe he should just come out and let her see exactly how stupid he was. "Y—yeah."

Her face twisted as she choked, "Peter, you don't want to be... to be married to me, do you?"

His courage sank at the sight of her horrified face. "Of course not. It's just that..." He suddenly remembered something. "It's just that my mother left me a message.

"Your mom?"

Out of the blue, Peter was hit with a blinding inspiration. He knew exactly what he should do. There was no way he could admit the truth to her right now. It was too new, too unexpected. Kelly wouldn't understand, and she wouldn't like it. Their friendship might not survive.

But maybe he could delay their annulment to give himself some more time. After being married to him for a little while, maybe Kelly would realize it wasn't so bad.

Maybe he'd have a chance to make this marriage more than an accident.

"Yeah," he said, holding his phone out. "She already found out about the marriage."

"What?"

"Heidi must have told her mom, who proceeded to tell everyone else in Savannah. Mom found out."

Kelly gasped and closed her eyes. *"Grandmama.* Grandmama must know by now. Oh, God, she'll never forgive me if I don't stay married to a Blake."

"My mom will be crushed too. She's been wanting me to settle down. I've already disappointed her enough. I hate to add something more."

Kelly was shaking her head. "I know it's terrible, but we can't stay married just so we don't disappoint our families. I mean, that wouldn't be right."

"No. It wouldn't be right. But maybe…" He didn't need to trail off. He knew exactly what he was going to say. He just couldn't sound too excited about saying it.

"Maybe what?"

"I think it would be worse if they knew it was just a stupid, drunken mistake. It will be easier to break it to them if they think we really tried to make the marriage work."

Kelly was frowning. "Maybe."

She wasn't buying it. He had to make it more convincing. "I don't know about your grandmother, but my mother takes marriage really seriously. She'll never accept that I gave up on a marriage without even giving it a try for a little while."

"So you think we should pretend to try for a little while?"

It did sound like a ridiculous scheme. An absolutely ridiculous scheme. And one he would never agree to if he hadn't had ulterior motives. "We don't have to," he said, trying to convey a sense of bleak resignation. "It's not fair to ask that of you, just to make it easier for me."

"I'll do anything you want to make it easier on you." Kelly's eyes were wide and earnest. "Seriously, Peter. If you think that would help you, I can pretend for a little while, as long as it doesn't go on too long. Neither of us should be trapped in this marriage for too long."

Trapped in the marriage. Evidently that was how Kelly viewed it. He ignored the pain in his heart to push on toward his goal. "It doesn't have to be long. Just a month or two would help."

"Okay." She was nodding, thinking hard, staring at a spot in the air. "That's okay. At least it would delay Grandmama's horror about my breaking up with a Blake. What about we stay married until after graduation. That would be a natural end point if we were going to call it quits for real. I counted the days up early this week. It's forty-five days now until graduation. We can give it that long and then get annulled or divorced."

Peter nodded. "Are you sure? I know it's kind of crazy."

"This whole thing is kind of crazy. I just want to make sure neither of us suffers too much because of it. So... so are we going to... to live together?"

"We'll have to," he said gently, starting to wonder if he was an asshole after all, tricking Kelly into something unfair. "It wouldn't be convincing otherwise. No, we shouldn't do this. It's not fair to you, to put you through this, just so that I can—"

"No! I want to. I want to do this if you think it's best for you. I don't mind moving into your place for a little while. We hang out there a lot anyway." Before he could agree to this, she gave a little jerk. "Wait, I can't leave Grandmama on her own. We'd have to live with her."

Peter gulped at the thought. "Okay. Whatever works for you."

"Okay. Surely it won't be too bad. If we're both practical and honest about it, I think we can get through with no problem."

"You're sure?"

"Yeah." She smiled at him. "I'm sure. Let's do it."

Peter was still conflicted, wanting it desperately but not sure if it was the right thing to do to Kelly, no matter how willing she seemed. But before he could say anything else, a phone started to ring from the main room of the suite.

Kelly stood up. "That's mine." She hurried into the room and picked up her phone from the floor. Peter stood in the bathroom doorway and watched as she checked the screen. "It's Deanna."

"She probably heard about us."

"Right." Kelly took a deep breath. "Okay. Here goes. Day One of a forty-five-day marriage."

Peter couldn't believe she'd agreed, and he couldn't believe she was so casual about the whole thing, as if it was a little game they were playing.

It was probably best she thought that though. She couldn't know how he felt.

She wasn't ready to know it yet. He would lose her for good.

At least this was something. He had forty-five days to win her over, open her eyes, make her fall for him.

Forty-five days was a long time.

Anything could happen by the end of it.

# FOUR

Kelly felt like a different person as she walked into her family home late that afternoon. There was no reason to feel that way since she'd been gone for less than two days. But the old house seemed smaller somehow, slightly unfamiliar, as if she didn't fit into it the way she had just the morning before.

She didn't like things to change. She especially didn't like to feel like *she* had changed.

She brushed off the feeling and smiled over her shoulder at Peter. "You ready for this?"

"Of course." Peter had been remarkably calm and casual about this whole situation. It was probably not as important to him as it was to her. She couldn't really be offended by this fact. He was her friend. He'd always been her friend. And once he'd grown accustomed to the idea, he obviously saw no reason to treat their current circumstances with anything other than his normal, reasonable friendliness.

If something in the back of her mind kept screaming at her that they were now married, Peter obviously didn't hear the same voice.

At the moment, he was looking around the grand entrance to the house—lovely polished staircase, newly restored chandelier—with a slight smile on his face. His brown hair looked almost gold in the sun from the windows, and he was lean and masculine in his jeans and T-shirt, a bag slung over one shoulder.

"Grandmama?" Kelly called out, trying to push the idea of how attractive he looked out of her mind.

She waited a minute and, when she heard nothing, gave a little shrug. "Maybe she's not in."

That would be good. It would give them a chance to get settled a bit before they faced her grandmother.

"Upstairs?" Peter asked, nodding toward the staircase.

"Yeah. My room is up there."

They both walked upstairs and turned to the right toward Kelly's room. When she opened the door, she stared inside at the small room. It was neat since she'd picked everything up before she'd left town. But the twin, four-poster bed in one corner looked even smaller than usual.

Peter arched one eyebrow. "You want us to live in here?"

She swallowed hard. Of course they would have to live in the same room since they were supposed to be married for real. But that would mean both of them would have to fit into that tiny bed.

A flush of heat washed over her at the thought.

Peter was peeking into the room next door.

"That's Grandmama's room," Kelly said.

His eyebrow lifted even higher. "Is there a room downstairs we could use?"

She almost chuckled at this expression. She could hardly blame him for not wanting to sleep right next door to her grandmother. Being in the same house would be intimidating enough. "Yeah. There's the guest room downstairs with a connecting bathroom. I guess we could sleep down there since it won't be for very long." She glanced over at her grandmother's room, feeling a sliver of worry. "If Grandmama needs me, she can call me downstairs or something."

"Does she need a lot of help at night?"

"No. She's really in pretty good shape for her age, but you know she fell last year and it took her a long time recover. I just worry about her being by herself."

"She won't be by herself." Peter put a hand on her upper arm. It should have been a casual gesture, but it felt strangely intimate. "We'll be in the house with her. We'll just be downstairs."

Kelly nodded, telling herself to be reasonable. Her grandmother was fine. They would all be fine. Peter would just be staying here for a month and a half, and then she could move back upstairs where she'd always slept. Things weren't changing permanently. She could easily deal with this for the next forty-four days. "Okay. Good. Let's go downstairs then. It's a really nice room. We completely redid the bathroom when we fixed up the house last year."

The guest room was immaculate, as it always was, with a beautiful handmade quilt in white and pale blue and antique mahogany furniture. Kelly tried not to focus on the bed, although she kept imagining what it would be like to sleep there with Peter.

They'd evidently spent last night together, but she couldn't remember anything about it.

"I can sleep here," Peter said, putting his bag down on the small settee next to the windows. It was about a foot shorter than Peter, with velvet upholstery and wooden arms and trim.

"You won't be able to fit!"

"Sure, I will." He grinned. "I don't want you to be uncomfortable, Kelly."

Even the sound of his saying her name made her feel ridiculously jittery. "I'm not uncomfortable."

"Yes, you are. You're trying not to look at the bed. I know you're doing this mostly for me, and I'm not going to make it any more awkward for you than I have to. I'll be perfectly fine here. You know, when I was traveling through Europe, I mostly slept on the ground."

He was still graciously taking the blame for the marriage, when Kelly knew very well that it was her own fault. "Okay. We'll see how it goes." She took a breath. "I guess I'll go get my stuff from upstairs."

"Okay. I'll go over to my place and bring back what I need for the next month." He stepped over very close to her, studying her face intently. "You're okay with this, right? If you're not, we need to put an end to it now."

She smiled at him in both self-consciousness and affection. She wouldn't have been comfortable going through this charade with anyone but Peter, but she would trust him in anything. She could trust him in this. "I'm fine. I'm not a child, you know."

"I know that." There was a timbre to his tone that made her shiver a little. Then he gave his head a little shake. "I'll be back in a little while."

She smiled again, but she felt strangely disappointed, like she'd missed something that might have happened a moment ago.

Walking upstairs, she told herself to get a grip.

Nothing really had changed. She was the same easygoing, no-nonsense person she'd been the day before. The most important thing to her still was her family, making sure she took care of her grandmother.

Peter was still her friend, even though he was temporarily her husband.

Nothing important about her life was different than it had been two days ago.

~

A half hour later she heard a sound from the front door, and she stepped out from the guest room, where she'd been folding some of her clothes in the dresser drawers.

Instead of Peter, Deanna walked in, looking pretty and breezy in a casual green dress and tall boots. In place of her normal smile, she was frowning as she put down her purse. "Where's Peter?"

"He's over at his apartment, getting some of his stuff."

"Where's Grandmama?"

"I don't know. She wasn't here when we arrived."

Deanna's frown deepened. "Oh, she said she was having tea with a friend this afternoon. So tell me what the hell is going on!"

Kelly sighed. She'd talked to her sister briefly on the phone that morning, but there hadn't been time or privacy to say much. "I told you before. Peter and I got married last night."

"But why?"

Kelly gave a little shrug. "Because we wanted to."

"But you always said you and he were just friends."

"We are. I mean, we were." She cleared her throat. "Things changed."

"So you really want this?"

"Why wouldn't I want this? Peter is great."

"I know, but this whole thing seems a little…"

"A little what?" It was ridiculous to feel defensive since everything Deanna suspected about the marriage was true, but Kelly still did. She wasn't a little kid. If she wanted to get married, she could get married—even if it was a sudden, drunken Vegas thing.

"A little irrational."

"Seriously? You married a man you barely knew because Grandmama bullied you into it. Rose got engaged to her boss to get him out of an awkward situation with his ex-fiancée. And you think *my* marriage is irrational?"

Deanna blinked for a moment, and then she burst into dry laughter. "I guess you're right. I was just worried that... I don't know how to explain it, but you seemed like you wanted to do... to be someone different the other evening. And I was just wondering if this was some sort of spontaneous way of doing that. I didn't want you to get stuck in a bad situation."

"It's not a bad situation. It's really not. It's Peter. It's *Peter.*"

Deanna scrutinized her face for a longer-than-normal length of time. Then she nodded, as if she was satisfied by what she saw. "Okay. I'll go along with it then."

"There's nothing to go along with," Kelly said, knowing as she said the words that they were futile. Deanna could obviously see that something was going on, something other than a normal marriage based in love. "We're married for real."

"I believe you." Deanna grinned. "Mitchell and I were married for real too."

"That's different," Kelly muttered. She suddenly wished that she and Peter could go away for the next forty-four days. It was so much harder to put on this ruse when surrounded by people who knew and loved them.

"Of course it is," Deanna replied.

Before Kelly could say anything else, the front door swung open and a small imperious woman with a steel-gray bun and a black dress stood in the doorway. Without even a greeting, she pronounced, "I had tea with Stella Blake."

Kelly tried not to groan. What the hell had her grandmother been doing with Peter's mother? "Did you?"

"Yes, I did. We are very surprised, but we have decided we will not object."

Kelly wondered silently what would have happened if one or both of the women had objected.

"We will have a wedding reception two weeks from tonight. It will be in Chevalier Hall."

Kelly tried not to make a face. "Peter and I don't want a big production or—"

"Of course there will be a big production. We will invite everyone. There will be no arguments."

Kelly met Deanna's eyes, and they shared a moment of frustrated understanding. Peter was going to hate this. He didn't want to rely on his family's money or connections. He didn't want the stuffy, artificial lifestyle of his parents. He certainly wouldn't want a fancy, pretentious party to celebrate his fake marriage.

But what could she do? Her grandmother would go through with this, no matter what she said. And she didn't want to hurt the old woman's feelings.

"Okay, fine." Kelly tried not to sound too annoyed. "Peter and I are going to stay here for a while, if that's okay. We can stay in the guest room downstairs." She made it sound like it was a favor, rather than the truth that she was mostly staying here to make sure her grandmother wasn't alone.

"That is acceptable. Now where is my new grandson?"

"He went over to his apartment to get his stuff."

"He will be here for dinner?"

"Yes, I'm sure he will be." Kelly cringed inwardly as she thought about eating dinner with Peter and her grandmother every night. That was sure to be awkward.

Maybe they could decide to go out to eat several nights a week.

~

When Peter had decided to use this opportunity to persuade Kelly to stay his wife longer than their agreed-upon month and a half, he hadn't counted on having her grandmother around all the time.

This was going to get old really quick.

He actually didn't mind the old woman. She was crazy, of course, with her old-fashioned ways of thinking and talking, with her obsession with her family history, and with her collection of stuffed Siamese cats. But he'd always found her rather amusing. Plus, Kelly clearly loved her, and that was reason enough for Peter to think well of her.

But he hadn't been living with her then.

From the moment he returned with his clothes and personal items, he couldn't seem to get away from her in the house. Even when he and Kelly were alone in their room, unpacking and organizing space in the bathroom and closet, he was aware of Mrs. Beaufort's presence. She was talking on the phone in the hallway right outside their door or puttering around in the garden, right outside the window to their room, or sticking her head into the room without knocking and asking Kelly to help her get dinner ready.

It was going to be a real challenge to romance Kelly with Mrs. Beaufort as an audience.

They ate dinner in the formal dining room at a huge table that was way too big for the three of them. Kelly was unusually quiet, and her grandmother quizzed him the whole time on his plans for the future and why he was so foolish as to not allow his parents to help him get started in the hospitality industry.

Peter replied as politely and patiently as he could, and he knew he'd behaved well when Kelly gave him a sympathetic smile, as if she understood how hard it was for him and she appreciated the effort.

After dinner, they all went into the "parlor" to drink hot cocoa and amuse themselves before bedtime.

It was only seven-thirty. Peter desperately wanted a television or his phone or a book or *something*. Instead, Mrs. Beaufort dozed by the fire while Kelly studied for an exam.

Peter didn't have any work to do for his classes. He only had two to complete before he graduated, and they were both general education requirements he could do in his sleep. He paced around the room for a while. Then noticed that the leg on one of the side tables was loose, so he fixed it, pleased with something useful to do. But when that was done, he paced some more, moving between looking out of the window and studying the creepy members of the Pride, Mrs. Beaufort's Siamese cats, which had each been stuffed and displayed upon dying.

He decided that he was going to have an early bedtime tonight. Maybe around nine.

"You can go to the room and watch TV if you want," Kelly said, glancing up and noticing his fidgeting.

"No, it's fine."

"He's a gentleman," Mrs. Beaufort said from her chair. Her eyes were closed, and it was spooky the way she seemed perfectly aware of her surroundings, even in her sleep. "He won't leave us yet."

"But he has nothing to do."

"Do you sing?" Mrs. Beaufort asked.

"No!"

"Play an instrument?"

"No, I'm not musical." He managed to temper his tone, although he was startled by the idea of singing or playing for this old woman's amusement.

"He could read a book out loud to us."

"Grandmama," Kelly said, a chiding note in her voice. "Don't be silly. Peter doesn't want to read out loud."

"I could if you really wanted me to." He managed not to sound too unnerved by the idea.

"Please don't," Kelly said, meeting his eyes, a flicker of amusement in hers. "It would distract me from my studying."

Peter sighed in relief. "Well, I don't want to distract you."

"Don't you normally work out or run in the evenings?" Kelly asked, setting down her book. "Why don't you go take a run or something?"

Peter glanced over at Mrs. Beaufort. "I don't want to be rude."

"You won't be rude." Kelly cleared her throat. "Grandmama? Tell him it won't be rude to go take a run."

Mrs. Beaufort opened her eyes just a slit. "Well…"

"Don't tease him. Tell him it's fine."

"Exercise would be acceptable," Mrs. Beaufort intoned.

Peter exhaled in relief, smiling over at Kelly and mouthing a thank-you.

She chuckled silently and picked up her book again as Peter got up to make a hasty retreat.

He changed clothes and then went outside to run through the historic neighborhood. It was a mild evening, and he had a lot of pent-up energy, so he ran for almost an hour before he finally returned to the house.

He was coming in the front door when he nearly ran into Mrs. Beaufort. She was evidently heading upstairs.

"Did you have a good run?" she asked.

"Yes. Thanks. Where's Kelly?"

"She said she was tired and so she went to her room. I am on my way to bed myself."

It was barely nine, but Peter wasn't about to complain about her early bedtime. "Okay. Goodnight."

Mrs. Beaufort took a step toward him, her expression changing. "Just a minute, young man."

Peter had been about to turn away, wanting to find Kelly, but he paused immediately at her words.

"What are you doing?" Mrs. Beaufort demanded.

"What do you mean?" Peter wiped sweat from his face. He'd felt pretty good until he'd come back inside. It was way too hot and stuffy in this house.

"What are you doing with my granddaughter?"

He blinked. "We got married. I thought she explained."

"Yes, she explained. But now I'm asking you. I want to know what your intentions are with her."

"My intentions?" It was like something out of an old-fashioned book. "I married her. I'm not taking advantage of her."

"Both are possible if this is some sort of a game you are playing with her."

Peter's heart was pounding, partly from his run but partly because of this conversation. He had no idea how she'd realized something wasn't right about their marriage, but she obviously knew there was more going on than they wanted to show to the world. "I'm not playing any games with Kelly. I wouldn't do that."

"Wouldn't you?"

"No. I wouldn't." He was a full foot taller than the old woman was, but it still felt like she was towering over him. He had no idea how she did it, but he would like to master the skill himself.

"Kelly is not as easy and casual as she might appear on the surface. She can be hurt. I will not let you hurt her. I don't care if you're a Blake. If you hurt her, I will crush you."

Peter was absolutely astonished. So astonished that he couldn't answer with anything but the truth. "I would never hurt her. I love her. I *love* her." He was dripping with sweat, and he felt like an absolute idiot.

But evidently his answer appeased Mrs. Beaufort. After another moment of cold scrutiny, her face relaxed slightly. "Very well. I expect you to be a real husband to her."

"That's what I want," he said, his mind whirling, trying to orient itself to this bizarre conversation. "That's what I want too."

"Very well." She gave a little nod. "Then go to her."

Peter stood like a statue while Mrs. Beaufort made her slow, dignified way up the stairs. Then he shook himself off.

Savannah definitely had the old lady wrong. Everyone thought she would do anything to marry her granddaughters off to rich men, men of good families. Yes, here she was, with Kelly married to a Blake, and she was doing her best to intimidate him and push him away.

She was trying to protect Kelly, and Peter couldn't help but like her better for it.

Mrs. Beaufort would have no way of knowing that protecting Kelly was the thing Peter wanted to do the most.

~

As Mrs. Beaufort predicted, Kelly was indeed waiting for him when he walked down the hall and into their large room.

She was sitting cross-legged on the bed, her textbook opened in front of her, but she didn't appear to be reading. She wore the two long braids she always wore, and she'd changed into a tank top and a pair of pajama pants.

She looked relaxed and beautiful, and Peter's heart did a silly little skip when he saw her. In bed. In their bed.

No, not their bed. He was sleeping on that little couch.

"How was your run?" she asked, pushing her glasses back up her nose as he entered the room.

"Good."

"Did you see Grandmama?"

"Yeah."

"Did she... did she say anything embarrassing?"

Peter wondered what she would consider embarrassing. "She wanted to know my intentions."

"What?" Kelly's green eyes widened, and she straightened her shoulders.

Peter tried not to let his eyes slip down to where he could see the outline of her breasts beneath her top. "She demanded to know my intensions. She didn't want me to hurt you."

Kelly's face twisted unexpectedly for a minute. "She thought you would hurt me?"

"I don't know. But she told me I better not." He gave her a little smile. "She really loves you."

Kelly looked down at her book, but he knew she wasn't seeing it. She gave a brief nod. "Yeah. But I thought she would jump at the chance of my marrying a Blake."

"Maybe she only wants you to marry whoever she picks out for you herself."

"Maybe. She was talking about Morris Alfred Theobald III earlier this week."

Peter scowled. "There's no way. He's like twenty years older than you. And he's awful."

"Don't look so outraged," Kelly said with a giggle. "She said he wouldn't be interested in me. Plus, I'm a married woman now, remember?"

He felt better at the thought. "Right." He wiped some more perspiration off his face. "I've got to take a shower. Do you need to use the bathroom before I do?"

"No. I'm fine. I put some clean towels in there earlier."

Peter went into the bathroom and got into the shower, cleaning himself up and telling himself not to get too excited about the prospect of going back into the bedroom with his wife.

She was sleeping on the bed. He was sleeping on the couch.

That was what they'd agreed to. That was the right thing to do.

He didn't get to sleep with her—touch her, kiss her, make love to her—just because she was his wife. No matter how much he wanted to.

He was confident that he was in control of himself when he went back into the room, wearing a T-shirt and pair of pajama pants. He preferred to sleep in just his underwear, but he was pretty sure that would make Kelly uncomfortable.

Kelly had turned the television on when he emerged from the bathroom, and she was flipping the channels.

"I thought you had to study," he said, trying not to look at her too closely. She didn't look the way she had last night—loose hair, sexy dress, seductive manner. She looked like normal Kelly—a fact that made him want her even more.

"I've studied enough. It's kind of early, but Grandmama won't go to bed until I do, so I always just go to my room early. I hope you don't mind."

"It's fine. I'd rather be on our own anyway."

Kelly had put a pillow, a sheet, and a couple of blankets over on the couch, so he went over to try to make a bed for himself.

"You're not going to be comfortable over there."

"I'll be fine."

"Why don't you come sleep on the bed with me?"

He desperately wanted to, but he also knew that would put him in a very dangerous position. Better to keep his distance until Kelly was more receptive to him. "I said I'll be fine."

"Well, you don't have to be grumpy about it."

He gave her a significant look. "I'll be grumpy if you don't listen to what I say. For the fifth time, I'll be fine sleeping here."

She made a face at him, but it was obviously mostly teasing. He stretched out on the couch, cringing as he realized how short it was.

He wasn't going to be able to sleep on this thing at all.

Kelly paused in her channel surfing to watch him as he tried to find a comfortable position. But there wasn't a position to be had. His head kept bumping against the wooden armrest, and his left leg kept falling off the narrow seat, and his legs had to bend up in unnatural positions to fit them in the short length.

He was very conscious of Kelly's observation. She seemed to be secretly laughing at him.

"It's rude to say I told you so," he muttered.

She chuckled softly, deliciously. "I didn't say a thing."

He sighed and let his head drop, knocking against the damned wooden armrest again.

"Would you stop being stubborn and get over here?" Kelly demanded after another minute. "There's plenty of room in the bed."

He sat up, trying to decide whether Kelly would really be okay with it. She sounded perfectly natural, like it wasn't a big deal at all, but she hid a lot that she didn't like to reveal to the world.

Not even to him.

"Besides," Kelly added, a lilt to her tone, "if Grandmama happens to peek in during the night, she'll be very upset to see you sleeping on the settee."

He gasped. "She's not going to peek in while we sleep, is she?"

Kelly burst into laughter.

He frowned as he stood up and walked over to the bed. "You shouldn't scare me like that."

She held down the covers to invite him in on the other side of the bed, and he reminded his body that this didn't mean what he wanted it to mean.

It was only when she was drunk that she'd wanted him for anything but a friend. She wasn't drunk now. This was real life. And she had no interest in him that way.

Yet.

Things could change. They had forty-four more days.

When he looked over at Kelly, she was smiling at him. "You're a real trooper to put up with Grandmama like this."

His breath hitched at the fondness in her face. "I don't mind. Really. You were joking about her peeking in on us though. Weren't you?"

"Of course." Her eyelashes lowered as if she were suddenly shy. Then she reached over and put her fingers on his shirt, very lightly. "I didn't realize you slept in pajamas."

"I don't normally," he admitted, giving himself a firm lecture about how, just because she touched him, didn't mean she wanted him to touch her. "I thought it might be more polite to wear more clothes though."

"Oh." Her mouth quivered. "So I shouldn't buy you some nice flannel pajamas for your birthday?"

He choked on amusement. "Please don't."

"Too bad." Her hand was still on him, resting gently on his chest. "Is it... don't you find it kind of strange, that we're married?"

"Yeah. I guess so."

"You seem like it's no big deal."

He couldn't tell if she wanted him to think it was a big deal or not. "Well, it's not as strange as I'd expect it to be. I mean, it's you. How bad can it be?"

He lifted her chin so she was meeting his eyes again, and her mouth widened into a slow smile.

He couldn't seem to pull his hand back, and they kept smiling at each other. And he was starting to wonder how wrong it would be if he just leaned over to kiss her.

She looked warm and soft and fond—like she really liked him. Maybe she wouldn't pull away.

Before he could decide, a clanging from somewhere in the house startled him so much he jerked, pulling his hand back like he'd just been caught doing something naughty.

"What is that?" he asked.

"It's Grandmama." Kelly was already getting out of bed. Her tank top had slipped down over one shoulder, showing more than it should have of her cleavage. "I gave her a bell to ring if she needed me."

"And she rings *now*?" Peter felt like a bucket of frigid water had been poured on his head. "What could she need?"

"I don't know, but I better go check on her."

Peter sighed as Kelly hurried out of the room, her slim body graceful, desirable, completely out of his reach.

He was never going to get Kelly to see him differently if they didn't have any privacy. She'd never agree to move out of her grandmother's house though. She was completely committed to taking care of her, and she'd never believe the old woman would be okay on her own.

Maybe they could get away for a short time. A honeymoon. That was what they needed.

After all, it would be completely natural to take a little honeymoon.

That would be perfect. Some time alone with Kelly so she could see he could be more to her than a friend.

He would think of something.

As long as Grandmother Beaufort didn't come with them.

# FIVE

The next morning Kelly woke up with the absolute certainty that something was wrong.

It didn't take her long to figure out what it was.

She was sleeping in the guest room downstairs, and the covers and pillow beside her showed clear evidence of someone having slept in the bed with her.

Peter.

The shower was running in the bathroom, so he must have already gotten up and was getting ready for the day.

She had an eight o'clock class today, and it was almost seven. She needed to get up pretty soon too.

Sitting up, she rubbed her face and straightened the straps of her tank top. Last night hadn't been as awkward as she would have expected. She and Peter had watched some TV, talked casually, and then eventually fallen asleep. She hadn't rolled over on top of him or anything embarrassing like that during the night. While she'd been brutally aware of his body right beside her, she'd managed not to act like she was particularly uncomfortable with the arrangement.

She'd have to keep up with the same demeanor. She couldn't let this fake marriage damage their friendship. It never would have happened at all if she hadn't gotten so wasted in Vegas, so she was the one responsible for ensuring that they got through it with as little difficulty as possible.

But it was so strange to think of Peter in the shower right now, rubbing his naked body down with soap. It gave her a jittery feeling that she really needed to get under control.

What he looked like in the shower was none of her business. She might be wearing his ring, but it was only for the next forty-three days.

The sound of spraying water stopped, which meant he was getting out of the shower. She forced herself not to visualize what he looked like, stepping out onto the bathmat, soaking wet, water streaming down his chest, his long legs, his face, his ass.

She was still trying to clear her mind of the visual a minute later when the bathroom door opened and Peter stepped into the room, wearing nothing but a pair of boxer briefs and rubbing his wet hair with the towel.

She stared, startled and hopelessly drawn to the sight of his lean body, tight muscles, firm flesh. Her eyes dropped unerringly to his groin, the outline of which was visible beneath the fabric of his underwear.

"Oh, sorry," he said, lowering the towel slightly as he saw she was sitting up in bed. "I didn't know you were awake."

Kelly told herself to stop looking at him, but her eyes completely ignored her mind. "I've got an eight o'clock class."

"I know that." He gave her that little arch of one eyebrow as he started towel-drying his hair again. "You think I don't know your schedule?"

"I know you know." She was starting to feel a little flushed as he turned around to lean over and open a drawer of the dresser. He had the best butt she'd ever seen on a man in her life. "I was just saying."

He glanced back at her over his shoulder. "You were just saying what?"

She had absolutely no idea what she was trying to say. "Nothing. Just that I always get up by seven."

She prayed the response was basically lucid, and was relieved when he turned back to pull out a pair of jeans without further comment. He worked at the hotel on Monday afternoons, but he always had time to come home to change after class into his work clothes.

She should be getting out of bed and heading into the shower herself, but she couldn't make herself move yet. It was so strange to watch him get dressed. It occurred to her that she should be polite and give him some privacy, but he was the one who had stepped into the bedroom in nothing but his underwear. If he'd wanted privacy, he should have dressed in the bathroom.

He didn't look remotely self-conscious as he pulled on the jeans. "What are you thinking about?" he asked, his eyes studying her face closely.

She really, really hoped he couldn't see what she'd been thinking about just now. She wasn't exactly aroused, but she was flustered and shivery and a little embarrassed. Something about seeing him like this was so intimate—more intimate than anything else she could remember.

To cover, she said the first thing that came into her mind. "I was thinking about the first time we met. Do you remember that?"

"Of course I remember that. You think I don't remember when I first met you?"

He looked almost offended, which confused her even more. "I just meant you might not remember all the details. Guys don't remember things like that, do they?"

He frowned, walking over to sit on the edge of the bed beside her, still bare-chested and now strangely intense. "It was a Monday, the first day of class in the fall semester three years ago. History of the Civil War. You were five minutes late and tried to sneak into the classroom without anyone noticing. You were wearing a blue shirt and your favorite jeans. You had to climb over me to get to the only empty seat in the class, and then Dr. Higgins said, since you were late, you could tell the class something interesting you knew about the Civil War."

Kelly's heart was doing the craziest gyrations in her chest as Peter spoke, his eyes resting on her face with something that looked fond, almost possessive. "You remember all that?"

"Of course I do. You proceeded to explain the whole history of Captain Beaufort in the Confederate Army. When Dr. Higgins asked how you knew all those details, you said you'd heard them as bedtime stories since you were four years old. I knew right then that I had to get to know you."

She was smiling like an idiot. "You only wanted to get to know me because of this old house. Don't try to pretend it was something personal."

"It was—"

"It was the house. The first thing you asked me after class was if I lived in the old Beaufort house and if we had any plans for restoring it."

"Well, I had to think of something to say. And I'd always thought it was a gorgeous old house." He was smiling too—just as much as she was. "But it was you I wanted to get to know."

"Don't try to make up stories now. I know the truth."

Something unexpected happened to his face. The smile transferred to a deep, almost serious expression. "I don't think you know more than the smallest sliver of the truth, Kelly," he murmured.

Her hands were trembling, so she had to hide them under the covers. If she didn't end this conversation soon, she was going to say something infinitely stupid, something she couldn't take back. "I know it's after seven now, and I'm going to be late for class if I don't get moving. I've got to make sure Grandmama doesn't need me to do anything."

"I'll drive you to class so it won't take you so long to get there."

She usually walked since the campus wasn't far and she didn't own a car. "But your class isn't until ten."

"Yeah, but I have a paper I need to work on anyway. I can just spend a couple of hours in the library."

"Okay. Thanks."

Peter stood up, and she thought he was going to finish getting dressed, but he stood looking down at her. After clearing his throat, he said casually, "I don't have to work this weekend, so I was thinking..."

When he didn't finish, she frowned. "You were thinking what?"

"Since people think we're married for real, it would make sense for us to have a honeymoon."

"What?"

"A honeymoon. Nothing big, but maybe we could go away this weekend. I think that would be a normal thing for a couple to do."

"Go away where?"

"I don't know. It doesn't matter."

"But anywhere we go would cost money."

"That doesn't matter."

She stiffened her shoulders. "Yes, it does. We just had that trip to Las Vegas. We can't go on another trip so soon. We don't have the money for it."

"I have the money."

"But you're saving your money to buy a property when you graduate. You can't go blowing it on something useless like a honeymoon."

"It won't be anywhere expensive. We don't have to fly. We can drive somewhere and get away. People aren't going to believe we're married if we're around your grandmother all the time. No newlyweds would want to do that."

"I don't care what people think. They'll have to deal with it. I can't leave Grandmama again anyway. And I'm not going to let you waste your money like that."

He was frowning now, and he looked as displeased as she felt. "It's my money. I can spend it however I want."

"Then you can go on a honeymoon by yourself."

"Kelly—"

"No, Peter. I'm not going to let this stupid fake marriage hurt you in any way. I'm not going to let it use up your savings or make it harder for you to find a good property when you graduate. You've worked too hard. I know how much you want this. I know how much it means to you."

"But it's not the only thing that means something to me."

She didn't understand what he meant by this—only that he was being stubborn about something ridiculous. She was about to reply when her phone chimed with a text. Reaching over to grab it from the nightstand, she read the message.

"It's Deanna," she told Peter. "She wants to know if we can have lunch today with her and Mitchell."

Peter looked surprised. "Sure. I guess so. What do they want?"

"I assume they want to check us out and figure out what's going on with us."

"You're not going to tell them the truth, are you?"

"No. No, of course not. Deanna might suspect something, but we'll just tell them it was spontaneous, and this is what both of us want."

"Okay." His face had relaxed, and he was smiling again as he pulled a T-shirt on over his head. "I need to be at work by two, but that should still leave us plenty of time for lunch."

Kelly let out a breath and made herself get out of bed. She'd known a temporary marriage like this would be awkward in a number of ways—even between her and Peter.

She had no idea why he'd gotten this silly idea about the honeymoon in his mind, but hopefully it was just a passing thought and he'd already let it go.

At least here, in her home, with her family, going to her regular classes, she could still basically feel like herself—even though she was married.

If she was alone with Peter for the weekend, as his wife, she'd start to feel like somebody different.

And then she might do something that Kelly Beaufort just didn't do.

~

Peter's class got out a few minutes early, so he walked over to the building where Kelly's class was held and waited near the door for her to come out.

They were heading over to the Claremont, the luxury hotel Mitchell owned, afterward to meet him and Deanna for lunch.

As he waited, he tried to think of who could spend the weekend with Kelly's grandmother so she couldn't use that as an excuse.

Peter knew Kelly cared about him. Genuinely. Strongly. But her affection for him still ran a distant second to her grandmother.

He couldn't even resent it. Kelly's love for her family was a deep part of who she was, and he wouldn't want her any other way. But her family circle was tight, very small. He would never be included in it.

But still, there must be some way to work around it. If they could get away for a few days, he'd have a better chance of introducing her to how much more could exist between them.

It might be a long shot, but at least it was something. As it was, nothing was likely to change.

He'd been leaning against a tree, but he straightened up when Kelly walked out of the building. She wore her braids and her glasses and a pair of worn jeans. She looked exactly as she always looked, but his heart still sped up at the sight of her.

He tried not to remember how rumpled and sexy she'd looked this morning as she sat in bed and watched him get dressed. For a few minutes he'd thought he was actually making progress. She'd looked flustered, self-conscious, like she was thinking about him, seeing him, in a different way. Then she'd been so sweet and affectionate as they'd talked about the first day they met. But the moment had been lost as soon as she'd remembered her grandmother might need her.

Kelly smiled when she saw him waiting. When she reached him, he spontaneously took her face in his hands and gave her a soft kiss.

For a moment, her lips, her body, melted against his, but then she stiffened up and pulled away. "What are you doing?"

"Kissing my wife."

"But why?"

"Because we're supposed to have just gotten married and that's what a husband would do."

"Yeah, but—"

"Aren't we supposed to make this convincing?"

"Yeah, but there's no one around here who—"

"You never know who might be watching. We should be careful."

He watched a series of emotions flicker across her face—annoyance, amusement, acceptance, resignation. "Fine," she said at last. "I guess that makes sense. Let's get going so we're not late for lunch."

He smiled as they started walking back to his car. "Is kissing me such a chore?"

"No!" She looked startled by her own vehemence. "It's just a little strange. I mean, we're not supposed to be kissing."

"I've never been married before, but I understand that kissing is a fairly common occurrence."

She chuckled softly. "Yeah, but we're just supposed to be friends."

It actually hurt a little, that she was so completely convinced of this, that it never seemed to cross her mind that they might one day be even more than friends. He pushed the feeling aside, though, and kept his tone light. "Not for the next forty-three days."

"Right." She gave him a little smile. "I'll try to remember that."

~

They had lunch on a private patio at the Claremont. The day was sunny, the food was delicious, and the ambience incredibly pleasant. Peter loved this hotel. Ten years from now he would love to own a place like this—with the same kind of attention to detail and skilled hospitality.

It had taken Mitchell about ten years. Peter was sure that he could do it too—even without relying on his family's money and connections.

Peter wasn't like Mitchell though. Mitchell was one of those guys who got through life by charming everyone around him, easing through difficulties with a way with words and a charismatic smile. Peter wasn't like that. People who knew him liked him, but it usually took him a while to warm up to others. His mother had always said he was too independent for his own good, that people recognize when you don't need them and therefore don't make an effort to know you.

She was probably right. He had plenty of friends, but people didn't fawn over him the way they did over Mitchell.

Peter could see it even now in the manner their server had toward Mitchell. She was scrupulously polite, but she watched him like he was a gift sent down from heaven.

When he saw Deanna frowning slightly as the woman retreated, after bringing out their lunches, Peter suspected that Deanna saw the same expression he had.

She turned toward him unexpectedly and must have caught the look on his face. She gave him a dry little smile. "I'm used to it."

Peter couldn't help but laugh. Deanna was a lot like Kelly in some ways—in that straightforward practicality and ironic, intelligent humor. She was pretty in an obvious manner, which wasn't as appealing to Peter as Kelly was, but she had the same sort of hardworking patience and commitment to family that all the sisters had.

They really were a remarkable family. And Kelly was the most remarkable of the three.

"Used to what?" Mitchell asked, lowering his fork before he took his first bite.

"Used to everyone drooling over my husband." Deanna gave him a teasing smile that made it clear she wasn't genuinely annoyed or resentful. "It's a cross I have to bear in long-suffering silence."

"You might want to remind yourself about the silence part," Mitchell teased, reaching over to cup his wife's face gently.

Any question Peter might have had about whether Mitchell's charisma really bothered Deanna vanished at the look on the man's face. She could have absolutely no doubts about how much her husband loved her. Peter was immediately uncomfortable, as if he'd intruded on a private moment.

He looked over to Kelly automatically, and their eyes met for a moment. He didn't have a chance to interpret the look in her eyes because she broke the gaze almost immediately.

"I thought *we* were supposed to be the newlyweds," she said in a bland voice.

Deanna laughed, and Mitchell dropped his hand. "That's right," he said. "What's that about anyway?"

"Crazy things happen in Vegas," Peter said, making sure to keep his voice light and mild.

"I guess so." Mitchell looked between the two of them. "You're not going to live in that old house for very long, are you?"

He didn't have to say it. Peter knew he was referring primarily to living with Grandmother Beaufort.

"It makes sense for now," Peter said since Kelly's eyes had flashed over to him. "At least until we graduate."

"What are you going to do then?" Mitchell asked.

"Peter is in hotel management," Kelly said. "He wants to do the same thing you do."

Peter would have said it differently, but he couldn't help but like the fond admiration on Kelly's face—as if she really appreciated his dreams for the future.

"Really?" Mitchell asked. "Why didn't you tell me before? I might be able to get you a position here if you're any good."

"He's great," Kelly said before Peter could respond. "He'd be amazing, working for you here. He's working at East Bourne House right now."

"Really? That's a good property." Mitchell pulled out his phone and appeared to make a note for himself. "Send me your stuff, and I'll take a look at it. When do you graduate?"

"In May," Peter said before Kelly could chime in again. She looked so pleased and proud of him that he could hardly begrudge her for interfering, but he felt incredibly uncomfortable by this conversation.

He didn't want to work for Mitchell any more than he wanted to work for his father. Whatever he did in life, he was going to do it on his own.

Searching for a diplomatic way to pull back some, he said, "I'm still figuring out what I'll do after graduation, but I sure appreciate the offer."

Mitchell nodded, as if the issue were resolved in his mind, and Peter saw Kelly and Deanna giving each other pleased looks.

He sighed.

Maybe his mother was right. Maybe he shouldn't be so independent. Maybe he should accept help when it was offered. It would make life so much easier.

But easy wasn't him. It had never been him. He'd resigned himself to that years ago.

"So how are things going?" Deanna asked, obviously making an effort to change the subject. "Living with Grandmama, I mean?"

"It's fine," Kelly said. "It's totally fine. We moved downstairs, so we have a little privacy."

"Not much," Mitchell muttered, a spark of amusement in his eyes. "Does it feel like those horrible cats are always breathing down your neck?"

Peter and Kelly laughed while Deanna gave her husband a glare of mock indignation. "Don't bad-mouth the Pride. You'll hurt their feelings."

"Their feelings—and their creepy, flea-ridden stuffed bodies—can all go to—"

"Hey!" Deanna cried, interrupting her husband. "They don't have fleas."

The laughter that followed faded pleasantly as they focused on eating their lunches for a couple of minutes. Until Deanna picked up where they'd left off, "But, seriously, if you ever need any help with Grandmama or anything, just let us know."

Peter could see that Kelly was about to say they were just fine, but it was too good an opportunity for him to ignore. So, before she could say anything, he put in, "Thanks. We appreciate that. Actually, I was hoping to take Kelly away for the weekend for a little honeymoon, but we weren't sure if we could manage it or not."

Kelly gave a little jerk and she widened her eyes at him, her surprise turning into a look that made it clear she wasn't at all pleased by what he'd said.

"Of course you need to have a honeymoon," Deanna said. "When did you want to go?"

"They're planning that reception for us next weekend, so this weekend is really the best time for us to go."

"That would be fine," Deanna said, smiling, as if she were really happy to be able to help. "Mitchell and I could come stay with Gran—"

Mitchell cleared his throat quite loudly.

Deanna corrected herself. "Grandmama could come stay with us for the weekend since Mitchell is allergic to the Pride."

"She doesn't like to leave home," Kelly said. "There's no reason why—"

"Of course there's reason," Deanna objected. "You've always taken care of her. You deserve to have a break."

"I had a break last weekend. I don't need—"

"You do need a honeymoon, and it wouldn't be fair for you two not to have one, just because you have the responsibility of taking care of Grandmama. I'll talk to her this afternoon. It will be fine. You guys definitely need to go."

Kelly's eyes were shooting daggers at Peter, and he knew he'd be in for it once they were alone together again. She wasn't happy with him. At all.

But he couldn't help but be relieved at the idea of a weekend away. Just with Kelly.

"Thank you," Peter said. "That's really great. I have to work Friday morning, but we could leave midafternoon. And we'd be back by the end of the day on Sunday."

"Where will you go?" Mitchell asked.

"I don't know. But we'll figure out something."

Kelly had arguments with Peter occasionally—usually just snippy little disagreements that were soon forgotten—but she couldn't remember ever being as angry with him as she was at the moment.

The asshole. She'd told him very clearly she didn't want a honeymoon, and then he'd went and engineered it anyway.

What the hell was he thinking?

She put on a polite manner and fake smile for the rest of lunch, but she was steaming as they walked in silence back to Peter's car.

She wasn't the kind of person who had a fiery temper. She didn't get angry very easily. So she wasn't used to the feeling of practically exploding from it.

Especially directed at Peter.

She shut the car door and buckled her belt, breathing heavily as she tried to control her feelings enough to form words.

Peter had buckled too and turned on the car, but he looked at her rather than shift into gear. "Just say it," he murmured, sounding resigned.

"How *could* you?" she snapped. "You knew—you *knew*—I didn't want to go anywhere, and you just did it anyway!"

"Why shouldn't I do something nice for us?"

She clenched her hands, more enraged by his calm look than she would have been by matching anger. "Because I told you I didn't want it."

"The reasons you didn't want to go weren't reasonable. It's my money. I can do what I want with it. And you have two sisters. You're not solely responsible for your grandmother's welfare."

"It doesn't matter whether you think my reasons are reasonable or not. All that matters is that I said no, and then you went ahead and did it anyway."

"I know you're annoyed, but it's not really that big a deal."

"Not a big deal? You think trampling all over my wishes isn't a big deal?"

He raised his eyebrows. Not his cute, one-eyebrow thing, but a rather cool, smug, two-eyebrow arch. "Since you've brought it up, you know very well that I don't want to go around asking people to help me in my career, and you did it anyway just now. How is that any different?"

She froze for a minute so surprised by the words that she couldn't fully process them immediately. "Seriously? You mean my mentioning to Mitchell that you want to go into hotels?"

"Yes. That's what I mean. I'm not going to accept charity from him, you know."

"It's not charity!" She seldom raised her voice, so she had no idea why she was now. "That hotel is his baby. He would never hire anyone unless they were the best. He's not going to give you a job just because you're my husband."

"Even so."

"Even so what? I thought you'd be happy. I was trying to help."

"I've told you over and over again that I don't want that kind of help. Anything I do, I want to earn on my own."

"I thought you meant from your family. You mean you don't want *anyone's* help?"

"Not like that. I don't want to be given anything."

He was the most infuriating man she'd ever known. She couldn't believe he was being so stupidly proud and stubborn. "Talk about unreasonable," she bit out. "That's the most unreasonable thing I've ever heard."

"I'm not expecting you to understand."

She was getting distracted from her anger because she was so confused and worried about this hang-up of Peter's. But his words brought her back suddenly to the issue at hand. "Okay. Okay. I don't understand your reasons. Then you better accept that you don't understand my reasons for not wanting a honeymoon. If you can be unreasonable about that, then *I* can be unreasonable about this."

Peter stared at her for a long moment, and she had no idea what was going on inside him. He looked deep and conflicted and angry and strangely helpless. Then he seemed to shake it all aside. "It's too late. Your sister is already planning to have your grandmother stay with them for the weekend. If you make a fuss about it, they're going to suspect that something is strange about our marriage. A normal wife would want to go on a honeymoon if it was possible."

He had her trapped. Absolutely trapped. If she was going to go through with this ruse, then she would have to go on the honeymoon. And, since she'd gotten Peter into this, she couldn't mess it up for him now.

She bit her lip and looked away from him, too upset to even speak.

He put the car into drive and started back to the house without another word.

There was no reason for Kelly to be so emotional. In the long run, it didn't really matter.

But she'd always believed that Peter really respected her. She couldn't believe he would just walk all over her that way.

And she couldn't believe he would shrug off her attempts to help him in his career—as if the fact that she cared about him meant nothing.

She stared out the window and tried to keep control of her feelings, telling herself over and over again that this wasn't as big a deal as she was making it.

When they got home, Peter put the car into park and turned in his seat to face her. "Kelly," he began, slightly hoarse.

She didn't want to hear it. She scrambled out of the car and hurried up to the side door that was closest to where they parked.

Peter was right behind her, and he caught her in the hallway. He grabbed her arm and turned her around to face him.

She tried to pull away, but it didn't work. She wasn't sure how it happened, but he had her trapped against the wall, one hand planted on the wall beside her shoulder and his body preventing her from moving.

"Let go of me," she gasped, squirming slightly. She was still angry, but she was more than that now. Her mind was spinning like crazy, bombarded with intense sensations from his body so close to her, the strangely passionate look in his eyes. "Grandmama's home. She can't see us fighting."

"I don't care if she's home." He spoke in a guttural tone that sent shivers down her spine. "You're my wife, and we need to talk."

"We already talked. You know how I feel. I'll go on this honeymoon because you trapped me into it, but I'm never going to be okay with you bulldozing over me as if my will means nothing. I can't believe you're one of those men."

He grew very still, the expression on his face changing almost imperceptibly. "You really think I'm one of those men?"

"I never did before." Her voice cracked, and she had to clear her throat to continue. She was shaking all over. She was never this way. She had no idea what was happening to her. "But you just... you just..."

"I really thought you'd like to go but were worried about the logistics. I didn't realize you actually didn't want to go on a trip with me."

His voice was even, but there was an underlying edge that made her wonder if she'd hurt his feelings. That idea upset her even more. "It's not that. It's not about that."

"Then what is it about?" He was still far too close to her. His face was only inches away from hers.

"I know it's not a real marriage, but whatever it is, I want it to be equal. I want to... I want to be heard."

"I do hear you, Kelly."

"Do you?"

"Yes." His face softened. "I'm sorry about the whole thing. I just had it in my head that this would be a good idea, and I didn't think you would really mind, once it happened. I'm sorry. I won't do it again."

She took a shaky breath, so relieved she was about to lose it. She was behaving ridiculously, but she couldn't seem to snap out of it. "Thank you," she whispered. "I know it's not a real marriage, but..."

Peter reached down to pick up her left hand and brought it up so she could see it. He twined the fingers of his left hand into hers so that the rings on their fingers were right next to each other. "It is a real marriage. It might be temporary, but we're married for real."

For some reason, the words, and the reality that they were true, were the last straw for her already battered emotions. A single tear slipped down her cheek. "I know."

He wiped the tear away with his right hand, very gently. "We don't have to go on the honeymoon if you don't want."

"No, we should do it now. It would be too complicated otherwise. It'll be okay."

"You're sure?"

She wasn't sure. With the way she was feeling right now, being alone with Peter for the weekend might be the most dangerous thing that could happen to her. But it was also something she desperately wanted. "Yes."

"Okay." For the first time since they'd entered the house, he gave her a little smile. "So we're okay?"

"Yeah. We're okay."

"Good. I'm not used to you being mad at me. I don't like it."

"I don't like it either."

"Let's not do it again then."

"Sounds good to me."

He was still holding her left hand as he leaned down to very softly press his lips against hers. It felt so good that, as he drew back, she leaned forward enough to claim his mouth again. Pleasure and excitement rushed through her as their lips moved together and his tongue made teasing little slides.

She was just about to wrap her arm around his neck when she realized what she was doing. She pulled away with a gasp. "What are you doing?"

His eyes were warm, almost amused. "I thought your grandma was coming."

"What?" She looked both ways down the hall. "She's not here."

"Yeah, but I thought she might be coming. I figured we better cover so she wouldn't know we'd been fighting."

Kelly frowned, overwhelmed with embarrassment as she realized how shamelessly she'd responded to the kiss, which was supposed to just be fake. "She wouldn't like us kissing any more than she'd like us fighting. She'd give you a lecture about being fresh with me."

"But we're married."

"That wouldn't matter to her."

His expression was warm and laughing now. "She'd really say fresh?"

"There are no limits to my grandmother's vocabulary when it comes to young men acting improperly."

He laughed. "I'll have to test that out then." Before she realized what he was doing, he leaned toward her again and gave her another soft kiss.

This time, when she got enough willpower to turn away, she saw in surprised dismay that her grandmother was actually standing in the hall, giving them a disapproving look.

"Disgraceful," Grandmama said, shaking her head. "I didn't realize my new grandson was such a rogue."

Peter straightened up, although he didn't release her hand. His eyes were laughing though.

Kelly was quite sure he'd never been called a rogue before. But then most men hadn't, until they'd encountered her grandmother.

# SIX

On Friday Peter and Kelly were on their way up to North Georgia, where Peter had found them a bed and breakfast on a lake.

The northern part of the state boasted hills and small mountains with a lot of scenic forests and waterfalls. There were plenty of B&Bs to choose from, but it had taken him a lot of time to decide on one since Kelly was so insistent that it wasn't expensive, but Peter still wanted to take them someplace nice.

He'd finally settled on one that had very good reviews but didn't look as fancy as the most expensive places. He really hoped she liked it. He had only one chance here for a honeymoon with her, and so every detail was important.

She'd been staring out the window, admiring the scenery. But, as if she'd read his mind, she turned to him and said, "I thought you'd just get a place on Tybee Island or something."

"Why would I do that?"

"I don't know. It's so close, and you could have found us something cheap there."

She obviously had absolutely no idea he was trying to make this weekend special. For her. For them.

Keeping a casual smile on his face, he said, "You said you liked the idea of mountains on a lake, so that's what you're getting."

"I just said it would be nicer for a vacation than Vegas. Not that you should go to so much trouble for a fake honeymoon."

"It's not fake." Before she could interpret this statement in a way that made her uncomfortable, he added, "We're actually taking the trip. We might as well enjoy it."

She smiled at him, straightening one side of her glasses. "It's nice of you to try to find a place I like."

"What else would I do?"

She was still smiling, but she glanced away as if she were self-conscious. Then her posture changed as she saw something out the window. "Oh, look! It's another place for sale. I bet that's another big old house."

Peter glanced over and saw the sign planted next to a long driveway that disappeared into the woods. "It's getting late. We can't stop to look at every house for sale on the trip. We've still got at least another hour."

"Okay."

He checked her face and, since she didn't look crushed, decided he wasn't going to cave and turn the car around. Kelly loved old houses as much as he did, and they'd had a really good time at the previous places they'd stopped—mostly old farmhouses in the middle of nowhere. They hadn't been able to go inside, of course, but they'd parked and walked around a few places that were obviously unoccupied.

But the sun was starting to set already, and Peter didn't want to make an idiot of himself, trying to find his way to the bed and breakfast on backroads in the dark.

The road made a wide curve, so he focused on driving for a minute. The road followed a line around a lake, which they could see as the trees on one side of the road started to clear.

"Peter!" Kelly breathed.

He turned his head at the sound of her voice.

She was staring out the window, something almost like awe on her face, and she pointed across the water of the lake. "Look. Do you think that's the place that was for sale?"

He slowed down and ducked his head slightly so he could see what she saw. It was a huge picturesque Victorian house, built next to the lake, framed by the trees of the woods behind it. It could have been an oil painting. The light and shadow came together perfectly, making it look like a house from one of his dreams.

He'd slowed down instinctively so he could stare until a car roared up behind them and laid on the horn, obviously annoyed by how slowly he was moving. He pulled the car over onto the shoulder and put it into park.

Kelly immediately climbed out of the car and stood gazing at the house.

"It looks huge," she whispered when he got out and walked around the car to join her.

"It is huge."

She wrapped her arms around her stomach as if she were hugging herself. "I want it."

Peter wanted it too. Viscerally. There was nothing in the world—other than Kelly—that he could remember wanting so much.

But it was probably mostly a trick of the light. Up close, it wouldn't be so perfect.

"Can we go back and look to see if that's the one for sale?" Kelly turned to look up at him, her expression hopeful.

So what if he looked like a fool, getting lost in the dark as they tried to find their B&B? He wasn't going to disappoint Kelly, not when she was looking at him that way. "Yeah. We better."

He knew this was mostly a game to her, checking out houses for sale and acting like there was any possibility that she might buy them in the future. Peter wasn't deceived into thinking she was serious about making a purchase. Even if she'd had the money, she would never leave Savannah. She would never leave her family. It would go against everything she was.

But Peter couldn't help but think about his savings account. It wasn't particularly flush, but he had enough to make a down payment on a place.

A house like that would be perfect for a bed and breakfast.

Kelly was visibly excited as they turned down the driveway, and she made a little squeal as they saw that the big lovely house was indeed the one for sale. Up close, it was clear that the house had seen better days. It was obviously unoccupied, and the grounds hadn't been kept very well. Piles of dead leaves covered the driveway, and one of the outbuildings had literally fallen down.

But the Victorian architecture was gorgeous and intricate, and Peter loved the house just as much as he had from a distance.

Kelly was starting to get out of the car almost before Peter put it into park. "Oh, my God, look at that porch!" She was running around the other side of the house as Peter was climbing out of the car. She called out, "There's a back porch too! And a balcony on both the second and third floors!"

Peter followed her, feeling just as excited as Kelly did. The house felt like an old friend. And it would be absolutely perfect for a bed and breakfast. One of those outbuildings could be converted to a separate cottage.

"It's called Eden Manor," she said, beaming at him when she saw him approach. "Don't you love it?"

"Yeah," he admitted. "I do."

She peered at his face and evidently recognized that he was serious. "It would be perfect for a B&B."

"Yeah. I was just thinking that."

"I wonder how much it costs."

"It doesn't matter. There's no way I can afford it."

"But it's not in great shape. They'd have to take that into account in the price."

"Yeah, but even if I could afford the down payment, I'd never have enough money to fix the place up." He sighed, trying to be as reasonable as he sounded but unable to keep his heart from racing. "Look at the siding. It's not just that it needs to be painted. A lot of this wood has rotted out. And that's just the outside. It would probably take a fortune to fix this place up."

Kelly sighed, but then she climbed the front steps and pressed her face against the window, using her hands to block out the reflection. "It doesn't look too bad inside."

He came up to look too and had to admit that the interior wasn't in as bad shape as he'd expected. "I can't afford it, Kelly. I'm going to have to start with something small and move up from there."

Her shoulders slumped, but she nodded, making it clear that she understood. "It would have been perfect for you."

It would have been perfect for *them*, but it was obvious that the possibility of making something out of this beautiful old house with him never even crossed her mind.

She came over to take his arm as they started back to the car. "It's not that far from Savannah," she murmured, sounding like she was talking to herself. "It would be easy to visit you here."

He took comfort in the fact that she obviously didn't like the idea of him living far away from her. "Eh. I'll probably stick around Savannah."

She smiled up at him, although there was something almost bittersweet in her expression. "There won't be anything so perfect there."

"How do you know?"

"Because there won't be anything this perfect anywhere else." She sighed and glanced back at the house. "What you need is an investor."

"If you're thinking about Mitchell or James, then just forget about it. I'm not going to take money from your sisters' husbands—not even to buy this property."

She had a thoughtful expression on her face as they got back into the car. "I know that. I wasn't thinking about them."

He frowned. "Who were you thinking about?"

She shook her head and gave him a wide smile. "It doesn't matter. We should get going, shouldn't we?"

Of course they needed to get going, but Peter couldn't help but wonder if she'd had a particular investor in mind.

~

A few hours later, Kelly came out of the bathroom ready for bed.

The bed and breakfast was pleasant, clean, and comfortable, and she was relieved that Peter hadn't spent too much money on the room. They'd obviously have to share a bed, but they'd been doing so at home now for the past few nights, and it hadn't been too strange.

It was actually kind of nice, going to sleep with Peter beside her, waking up in the middle of the night and hearing him breathe. She'd never slept with someone like that before, and she hadn't expected to find it so comforting.

If occasionally she found herself all hot and bothered about being so close to Peter when he wasn't wearing many clothes, then she was doing a decent job of keeping that a secret.

It was nice to have a husband. And even nicer that it was Peter.

She wore a thin camisole—a little prettier than the tanks she normally slept in—and a pair of pale blue cotton pajama pants. She'd unbraided her hair and brushed it out loose, and in the bathroom she'd had the silliest desire to wear some sort of slinky nightgown to make herself pretty, sexy. For Peter.

Obviously, that was out of the question, but she was still intensely aware of Peter watching her as she walked to the bed.

He'd been doing something on his phone while she was in the bathroom, but he put it down now to get ready for bed himself.

There was only a small television in the room, but it was after ten in the evening, so she didn't feel the need to kill time with TV. After they'd arrived, they'd unpacked and walked around the grounds, and then they'd gone back to the house to have a glass of wine with the owners and a couple of the other guests. It had been a nice evening, and Kelly was happy as she climbed under the covers and turned out the lamp on her nightstand.

She heard Peter in the bathroom. He was obviously taking a shower. He always took a shower before bed. She couldn't help but like how clean and fresh he smelled when he got into bed afterward.

She got so excited waiting for him to come out that she had to tell herself to get a grip.

In about ten minutes he came out of the bathroom with damp hair, wearing nothing but a pair of gray pajama pants.

Instead of the normal shiver of appreciation at the sight of him, she felt the oddest clench—of her heart, her whole body. The feelings shouldn't go together—since they were contradictory. But she felt both of them at the same time. Longing. And possession.

Peter was her husband. Only hers.

And she wanted him so much.

He smiled when he saw her looking at him. "You need anything?"

"Nah. I'm kind of tired."

"Me too." After putting his phone on the nightstand, he turned off the light and got into bed beside her.

He smelled just as he always did—like the soap he used. She found herself moving toward him unconsciously.

"What are you thinking about, all intense like that?" he asked, sounding genuinely curious.

It would be easier if he weren't so observant, if he didn't know her quite so well. "I'm not intense."

He chuckled and reached an arm out, drawing her closer so she was right beside him. He didn't usually do that. He'd never done that. They always stayed safely on their own sides of the bed.

But she wanted to be close to him—so much that she couldn't roll away, no matter how much wiser it would be. She let out a breath and lifted one arm to rest it on his chest.

His manner was still casual. He wasn't making a move on her. He was just being companionable or something.

She liked it. A lot.

He kept his arm around her as he said, "I don't know why you try to lie to me."

She had to think back to remember what she'd said. "I wasn't all intense," she objected, when it came back to her.

"Yes, you were." He stroked her hair gently. Since it was loose, it was covering the length of her back. His touch felt incredibly good. She had the silliest desire to purr. "What were you thinking about?"

She sighed. She wasn't going to tell him the whole truth, but she could tell him at least part of it. "I was just thinking about how strange it is to be married."

"I don't think it's been so bad." His body had tightened slightly. She could easily tell since she was pressed up against it.

"I didn't say it had been bad. Just strange. Different."

There was a pause before he answered. "Yeah. It has been different. For sure."

"Do you think we'll be able to go back to being friends—afterward, I mean?"

"Why wouldn't we?"

"I don't know. Sometimes… things get in the way."

"I don't see why anything needs to get in the way of us. I'm not going to let you slip out of my life, even if you feel embarrassed."

She liked the sound of it. She liked the idea of his holding on tight, not letting her get away. Not that she wanted to go anywhere. "I'm not embarrassed."

Peter chuckled, still stroking her hair. "Sometimes you are. You were when I came into the room just now."

It was better that he thought she was embarrassed than that he know she was thinking about sex. "Well, it's just different, seeing you in your pajamas."

He didn't answer. For a moment she felt a strange tension from him. She didn't understand it, but it went away almost as soon as she recognized it.

She felt his body relax as he adjusted his arm, making her more comfortable against him. She should probably roll away, but she didn't want to.

"Things feel different in a lot of ways," she said, following the course of her thoughts.

"What does?" He sounded slightly tense again.

"Just things. I do, I mean. It's so strange to come here where no one knows us, and they all think it's perfectly normal that we would be married. They don't look at us like we're crazy or too young or not thinking clearly or not right for each other. It feels strange to me to be just a normal woman, who might be married to you."

He lifted her head so he could see her face, whatever was visible in the dark room. "Why wouldn't you be a normal woman?"

"I didn't mean I wasn't a normal woman. I've just always been the youngest, the one everyone knew would never get herself a man."

He frowned. "But you did that on purpose, right. You always made sure your grandma wouldn't try to match you up with anyone."

"I know. But I've done it so long that it's kind of become part of me. And it just feels strange that people would look at me and think something else." She sighed and lowered her head again, resting it against the side of his chest since she was still tucked up in his arm. "I'm probably not explaining it well."

"No, I think I get it. I'd always been a Blake growing up. I mean, that was the only way people saw me. So it was so strange when I took off and went to Europe, and no one had any idea who I was. I could be anyone. It was strange—and incredibly freeing."

She nodded, swallowing over a swell of feeling at how perfectly Peter had understood her. "Yeah. It's just like that. Why shouldn't I be just any woman on a honeymoon with her husband?"

"You can be. You can be that woman. You can be anyone you want." Peter's voice now had a rough texture that she liked.

She liked it a lot.

She wanted to keep talking, but she was suddenly afraid of how intimate it all felt. She really needed to be careful, or she'd start getting ideas that would just leave her crushed.

They were already a week into their six-week marriage. And no matter how much she might want to be this new woman, she was still Kelly Beaufort. Her life was in an old house in Savannah. Her family needed her, and she was never going to let them down.

She could play at being someone else for a few weeks, but she had to remember that it had a definite end date.

And she didn't want to have a broken heart at the end of it.

~

Peter stayed awake long after Kelly fell asleep.

She'd felt so soft and clingy as they were talking that he'd started to have some hopes that the evening could turn in a particular direction. But it obviously never crossed her mind.

She liked to be close to him. That much was clear. But she didn't want it to go any further than a tame cuddle.

He told himself it was natural after being just friends for so long. She wasn't going to want to jump into bed with him without warning—just because.

But it was getting harder and harder to spend the night in bed with her and not be able to touch her the way he wanted.

His body definitely didn't appreciate it, no matter how he tried to prepare himself in the shower before he got into bed.

He liked to hold her in his arms, though, even if it eventually became torturous, so he didn't let her go, even after she fell asleep.

She was starting to recognize that things were different. She'd admitted it herself. Maybe he wasn't as far away from what he wanted as he feared.

He tried to think through a strategy, but his mind instead went on flights of fancy. He imagined living with Kelly in that big Victorian house, turning it into a bed and breakfast, waking up to her smile every morning, sleeping with her every night, being allowed to take her the way he wanted.

His brain got lost on that path for too long until his body started to misinterpret the feel of Kelly against him. It felt like he was surrounded by her, her softness, her scent, her hair.

Even when he grew aroused, he couldn't yet bring himself to let her go. It was a sweet kind of torture, his body throbbing for her, knowing he couldn't have her.

Eventually she started to shift in her sleep. He wondered if she was dreaming. Then she started to move her hand on his chest in clumsy little grips. She made a few wordless sounds and kind of rubbed herself against him.

He groaned out loud. He couldn't help it. He wanted to feel her like that so much.

After a minute he realized that he couldn't do this—get off on the feeling of her moving against him, when she was asleep and completely unconscious of it.

He groaned again as he very gently dislodged her arm and rolled away from her.

He felt cold and empty and pained as he heaved himself out of bed and walked quietly to the bathroom.

It was his own fault though. He'd wanted to enjoy holding her in his arms, and now he was paying the price.

At least she hadn't been awake to witness the effects.

# SEVEN

The following evening, Kelly was sitting up in bed again, waiting for Peter to come out of the bathroom.

She was chatting with her sisters in a group text message. They wanted to make sure she was having a good time and everything was going well with Peter.

It *was* going well. Really well. Kelly couldn't remember when she'd had a better day.

They'd had a relaxing morning and a delicious breakfast. Then they'd gone hiking up to see a couple of the waterfalls in the area. On their way back, they'd stopped to look at a few more old houses for sale, and then they'd spent the rest of the afternoon taking it easy on the grounds of the bed and breakfast.

There was a bench swing next to the lake, which they'd sat in for more than an hour.

It felt kind of like a real honeymoon. Kelly felt happy, relaxed, really close to Peter.

And she wanted to be closer still.

Reminding herself for the hundredth time that they were just friends wasn't helping at all anymore. She wondered what Peter would do if she just jumped him as soon as he walked out of the bathroom.

She didn't, of course. He walked out in his pajama pants, with bare chest and bare feet, and her heart did a silly little skip while the rest of her body clenched in excitement.

Even more when he smiled at her.

"Are you tired?" he asked, walking over to the table where he'd left his phone.

"Not really. It's been a really great day."

His smiled warmed. "Good. I think so too."

Their gazes held for a minute, and then she started to feel awkward and nervous, so she reached over to the television remote. "I guess we can watch some TV if you don't want to go to sleep right away."

He cleared his throat as he climbed into the bed beside her. "Sure."

She turned the television on and started flipping channels, but nothing she saw held much interest to her.

When she landed on a commercial for personal lubricant that was supposed to transform regular sex into high drama, complete with rousing orchestra and fireworks, she glanced over at Peter, trying not to imagine herself trying out that lubricant with him.

He gave her his little eyebrow arch. "If you're looking for a testimonial, you're out of luck. I've never tried that stuff."

She burst into helpless giggles. "I wasn't asking!"

"My mistake."

"I wonder how many people go out and buy it, hoping their ordinary sex life magically transforms into mind-blowing pleasure."

"You've never been tempted?" The timbre of his voice shifted slightly.

She knew very well she should redirect the course of this conversation. She and Peter didn't talk about sex, and they definitely shouldn't start now. Not when he was in bed with her, half-naked and sexy with slightly rumpled hair and that clever amusement in his eyes. But she heard herself saying anyway, "Well, I don't have a sex life—ordinary or not—that needs transforming."

She stared at the television as she realized what she'd just said, torn between a rising excitement and embarrassment.

From her peripheral vision, she saw Peter turned his head so his eyes rested on her face. "No sex life at all?"

She was sitting up in bed, just like he was, but she pulled the covers up over her a little more. "Well, not currently. But it's not like I'm a virgin or anything though."

"You're not?"

Despite her self-consciousness, she looked over to meet his eyes. "You thought I was?"

"I didn't know. I wondered. You haven't dated anyone since I've known you, so I thought it might be a possibility."

Of course he'd wondered. Everyone probably wondered. Poor, boring, undesirable Kelly. "I haven't dated anyone—ever really. But I did have sex before."

"How did that happen?" He sounded like he really wanted to know.

There was no reason not to tell him. She'd told him almost everything else. "I was sixteen. He was part of the group of friends I hung out with in high school. We never really dated, but we started hanging out alone more. And then we... we just had sex."

"You don't sound like it was something you wanted."

She heard the caution in his tone, and she straightened up immediately. "It wasn't like that. Nothing like *that*. I did want to do it. I mean, I thought I did. We had sex four times, and every time I was a willing participant. It just... it just wasn't very good."

"Well, you both were sixteen. What did you expect?"

She gave a soft chuckle. "I know. I just thought it would be... be different. But it was always over before I could really process it. We'd be playing video games or something, and then he'd start kissing me, and then before I knew it, my pants were off and it was happening and then it was over. And afterward I would always get this sick feeling, like I wished I hadn't done it."

"Why did you?"

"I... I don't know. I liked him, and I thought it was something I wanted to do. After the fourth time, when I still had that sick feeling afterward, I told him I didn't want to have sex with him again."

"And let me guess," Peter said dryly. "He stopped hanging out with you."

"Yeah."

"Asshole."

She laughed again. "Anyway, pretty soon I had too much else to worry about, with my grandmother and our depleted finances. And I always had to make sure she didn't think I was appropriate marriage material, so I never put myself out there at all. So that's been my whole experience with sex. Pretty exciting, huh?"

"You were sixteen. I don't think most teenagers are having sex much more exciting than you had."

"You don't think?" She gave him a teasing look, feeling better now that she'd told him, like it wasn't really something to be embarrassed about. This was Peter, after all. "I suppose you were some sort of stud having mind-blowing sex at sixteen?"

He gave a huff of amusement. "Uh, no."

"So you had boring sex that was over before it started too when you were sixteen?"

"Something like that."

There was an uncharacteristic reticence in his expression that made her immediately curious. "Peter? What kind of sex were you having at sixteen?"

With a sheepish smile, he admitted, "I wasn't having any sort of sex. I didn't have sex until I was seventeen."

"Really?"

"Why are you surprised?"

"I don't know. You're just so good-looking and... and amazing I assumed you'd started early."

Pleased surprise washed over his expression, and he reached out to pull her against him in a one-armed hug. "Thank you. That's the nicest thing you've ever said to me."

She felt good—and a little embarrassed—but she stayed cuddled up against him. "So who was the first girl you had sex with?"

"My prom date."

Ridiculously, a little sliver of jealousy jolted through her. "Was she the first one you wanted to have sex with?"

"Of course not."

"So why didn't you start earlier?"

"I don't know. I was a kid. I wasn't all that confident around girls."

"Really? I thought you'd be a stud."

His arm tightened around her, and he nuzzled her hair very lightly. "I've never been a stud."

"Oh. I thought you were."

"Thanks."

They didn't say anything else for a few minutes, and the only sound that broke the silence was the babbling of the television, which she'd left on a repeat episode of a crime drama.

She wondered what Peter was thinking, whether he felt as close to her as she felt to him, whether he wanted to have her this close to him, whether he wanted to be even closer.

His arm around her felt like more than just a friendly thing. Maybe it was. Maybe his feelings were changing, just like hers were.

"Peter?"

"Yes." The one word was hoarser than it should have been.

She was about to ask him what he was thinking when a flare of fear held her tongue. What if she was wrong? What if she humiliated herself? What if their friendship wouldn't survive her making a move on him?

"What was it, Kelly?"

She let out a long breath. "Nothing really."

"Tell me what you wanted to know."

Put on the spot and suddenly terrified by the idea of everything changing with Peter, she fumbled through her mind for an appropriate question. "I was just wondering what happened between us that night in Vegas."

There. That had been a good cover. It was right in line with their conversation earlier, but it wasn't nearly so revealing, so vulnerable, as what she'd actually been wanting to ask.

"Oh." He shifted against the headboard, although his arm was still around her.

"I mean, I know we got married, but what happened between us in bed? You said we didn't have sex."

"We didn't."

"But something happened, didn't it?"

"Yeah."

When she glanced up at his face, she saw he was avoiding her gaze, which was unusual enough to pique her curiosity. "Peter? Did something bad happen?"

"No, no. Nothing really bad. Just... just embarrassing."

Her cheeks burned slightly at the idea of how uninhibited and foolish she must have been. "I know I probably made an idiot of myself. I was totally drunk. You don't have to be afraid to tell me."

"Oh, no. I didn't mean it was embarrassing for you. For *me*, I meant."

"What could you have done that was so embarrassing?" Her eyes were wide as she pulled away from him enough to turn her upper body and face him.

"The obvious thing." He was meeting her eyes now, only occasionally glancing away. "We... we started to consummate our marriage. You were touching me and then it was... it was over before we got anywhere."

She suddenly realized what must have happened, a wave of heat and excitement washing over her as she visualized it. She desperately wished she could remember what it had felt like to touch him that way. "Well, you were drunk too. It's nothing to be embarrassed about."

He gave a dry chuckle. "It's definitely something to be embarrassed about—although it's just as well it happened. I would have felt terrible if we'd actually had sex while you were too drunk to say no."

He was serious about that. She could see it on his face. And her head, her heart, her body were all roaring with how much she wanted him. She couldn't seem to hold back anymore.

She reached over and brushed a loose piece of hair off his forehead. "What makes you think I would have said no?"

He blinked, his body suddenly going very still. "Wouldn't you?"

She shook her head, throwing caution and wisdom and all good sense to the wind. "I don't know about then. But... but I wouldn't say no now."

He made a little noise in his throat, still holding himself perfectly still. "You mean you'd want to..."

He looked so surprised that she was immediately terrified she'd made a fool of herself after all. "I totally understand if you don't want to—"

"Don't want to?" His voice was no more than a rasp. "You think I don't *want* to?" Finally he moved, reaching out to take her hand and move it down under the covers to his lap.

She gasped as she felt that he was hard beneath his pants. Hard. Aroused. For *her*.

His eyes closed as she moved her hand against the length of him. And when he opened them again, his gaze was hot and intense and almost wild. He took her face in both of his hands. "Kelly," he murmured, just before he kissed her.

He pushed her backward with the force of his kiss, and soon she was on her back, with Peter on top of her, kissing her deeply, hungrily, desperately.

She was responding in kind, wrapping her arms around his neck and rocking her body up into his. She could barely see, barely think. She couldn't do anything but feel. And she was feeling so much—pleasure, excitement, joy, surprise— there was no way to process it.

But this was exactly what she wanted to do, and by some sort of miracle, Peter wanted it too.

He kissed her until her head spun, and then his hands started to roam over her body until she was almost dizzy from the sensations. He pulled her camisole up over her head, and his eyes went even hotter as he stared down at her naked body.

"Peter," she said, arching up slightly, her body out of control, even while a wave of self-consciousness overtook her.

"God, Kelly, you're... you're... so..." He cupped one of her breasts, and then he tweaked the nipple between his fingers.

She cried out in response, wondering if anything had ever felt so good. But she managed to ask, "I'm so what?"

He met her eyes. "You're so... everything I want."

He couldn't have said anything else that would have thrilled her more. She pulled his head down into another kiss.

When he finally pulled away from her mouth, he trailed kisses down her neck until he'd reached her naked breasts. He gave them each attention—more eager than skillful—but his ministrations were so effective that soon she couldn't stay quiet. She writhed and moaned and scratched his back with her nails until he finally raised his head and smiled down at her.

"What are you smiling about?" she asked, able to focus again at the break in sensations.

"Why wouldn't I be smiling?"

"Well, you don't have to look smug about it."

"Do I look smug?"

"Definitely."

"I'll try to work on my expression then." He was still smiling—soft and fond—as he leaned down to kiss her again.

She sank into the feeling of how much he seemed to want her, how much he seemed to care about her, how much he seemed to want to be with her this way.

When his mouth moved down to her breasts again and flicked her tight nipple with his tongue, she cried out loudly at the jolt of pleasure.

"Peter, I'm dying here," she gasped, sliding her hands down to clutch at his ass, feeling him through the fabric of his pants. "I'm not used to this."

He lifted his head immediately and appeared to check her expression. Then he relaxed into a smile. "What aren't you used to?"

"Being tortured like this."

"I want to make sure it's better than your teenaged sex."

It was so sweet that he meant it, that he was serious about making this good for her.

"It's already light-years better than that. If you don't make me come soon, I'm going to scream."

"Is that a promise?"

She started to respond, but he lowered his mouth to her breast again, suckling until she was rocking wildly beneath him and babbling out all kinds of helpless sounds.

Then she felt his hand beneath the waistband of her pajamas, sliding under her panties, touching her where she was so hot and wet and needy.

She almost choked as he slid a finger and then two inside her, her vision blurring as she clutched at his hair.

He teased and mouthed one breast as he pumped his fingers, and it didn't take long until her body was shaking helplessly as an orgasm broke over her.

The power of it shocked her, and she was breathless, wordless, as her body finally started to relax. Peter had lifted his head so he could watch her, but she was too overwhelmed to pull herself together, even knowing he was witnessing how hard she'd come for him.

He was stroking her face, his eyes resting on her possessively, when she finally found her voice again. "Give me a minute," she gasped. "And then you'll get a turn too."

He smiled and straightened up. "Take your time. I better get a condom anyway since I assume you're not on birth control."

"I'm not."

He stood up, and she was able to focus enough to feel a little thrill at how obviously aroused he was. The outline of his erection was clearly visible beneath his pajama pants, and he moved awkwardly as he walked over to his suitcase.

"You brought condoms?" she asked when he returned to the bed with a few packets in his hand.

He reached for the remote so he could turn off the television. "Of course. It's our honeymoon."

She chuckled, reaching out for him. "Good thinking."

He moved into her arms, kissing her deeply, with that same intense passion until she was excited again, running her hands over him eagerly.

In a clumsy rush they took off the rest of their clothes, and she reached for his erection excitedly. He groaned as she caressed him, and she would have continued if he hadn't suddenly rolled over on top of her.

"Hey!" she gasped.

"Sorry. But we're not going to have that same ending this time, and if you did that anymore, I was going to lose it."

She smiled, delighted by the idea of his being so into her that he would lose it just from the way she'd been caressing him. "Okay. Then let's go for a different ending this time."

He was smiling back at her as he reached for a condom, opening the packet and rolling it on. And he was still smiling at her as he positioned himself between her legs and nudged her thighs apart to make room for him.

Then he was slowly entering her, and it was so full, so tight, that she lost her breath. It was actually uncomfortable at first, but she fought to relax her body, overwhelmed by the tension on Peter's face that clearly showed how much he liked the feel of being inside her.

"You okay?" he asked hoarsely when he was able to open his eyes.

"Yeah." She shifted, realizing that the discomfort was gone and the sensation of him inside her was deep and full and good. "Really good."

"Good."

He leaned down to kiss her gently before he started to move. His rhythm was slow and steady at first, allowing her to rock her hips and figure out how to meet his motion. But it wasn't long before he was starting to pant and accelerate his speed.

She wrapped her arms around him and hung on as he took her faster, obviously losing himself in the sensations. His eyes never left hers, and she couldn't possibly doubt how much he wanted this.

How much he wanted *her*.

It was a heady feeling, almost as heady as the feel of him moving inside her.

They rocked together eagerly until the bed was shaking slightly, and both of them were panting loudly. It all felt incredible, and she couldn't hold back a few moans of pure pleasure as his rhythm intensified. The tension in his body was so tight it was shuddering through his muscles, and she could see the exact moment when he finally lost control.

It was like nothing she'd ever experienced, the sight, the feel of his climax, the way the waves of release washed over him, making him freeze and then moan.

When his body finally relaxed, he bent his elbows to lower himself over her. She held him tightly as he pressed clumsy kisses against her skin.

She couldn't believe she'd just done this with Peter. She couldn't believe how completely both of them had lost control.

And she couldn't believe how much she wanted to do it again.

She always wanted to be this close to him.

When he finally picked himself up to take care of the condom, he was watching her closely.

She smiled at him. "That was way better than teenage sex," she said, pleased that her voice was almost light.

He grinned back at her. "That was way better than any sex I've ever had."

It was the truth. She could see it in his face. "Maybe that's because you've never been on a honeymoon before."

~

Peter had to take a minute in the bathroom to pull himself together.

He'd managed not to lose it physically, but his emotions were completely out of control.

This was exactly what he'd wanted, but he still couldn't really believe it was happening. And underlying the surge of joy and pleasure was a little sliver of fear—that this could all be taken away, that she might change her mind, that it didn't mean to her what it meant to him.

She wanted to have sex with him tonight, but that didn't mean she would always want it.

And it didn't mean she was in love with him.

So he splashed water on his face and breathed deeply until he felt like he could think reasonably again. Then he went back into the bedroom.

Kelly was still lying under the covers. She smiled at him from the pillow, her hair in a messy tumble around her face and shoulders.

At least she was smiling. At least she hadn't immediately pulled back.

"So what do you think?" he asked softly, going over to sit down on the bed beside her.

"About what?" She must be feeling a little nervous since her expression was hesitant beneath her smile.

"You know what."

"I'm not sure... I'm not sure how that even happened."

He couldn't just burst out how helplessly he was in love with her. She wasn't ready to hear it. She would get scared and pull away from him. He had to be so careful. "I think it was probably natural. We've always been close, and now we're married."

"But I didn't think you were even attracted to me."

"Well, that's crazy. Of course I'm attracted to you."

She blushed slightly. "I didn't know that."

"I know you didn't. I didn't want it to complicate our friendship."

"But this is going to complicate it, isn't it?"

"I don't know. It doesn't have to."

Her smile faded. "So this was just a one-time thing that didn't mean anything?"

"Is that what you want?" He wasn't sure what he would do if she said yes. He would probably have to drink himself into a stupor.

"No. Not really."

He let out a breath. "Me either. So let's just see what happens." Finally able to relax, he got into bed beside her and stretched out.

She rolled over to look at him. "I don't want anything to get in the way of our friendship, Peter. You mean too much to me."

"You mean too much to me too. We'll just agree that our friendship has to survive, no matter what else happens."

"Are you sure?"

"I'm sure."

She trusted him. He could see it in her face. "Okay. Then we'll definitely stay friends and the rest we'll just play by ear."

It was as good as he could hope for. He reached out and pulled her into his arms, relieved when she nestled against him.

He enjoyed holding her that way until both of them dozed off. When he woke up again, it was still dark in the room, but he had the strongest feeling that Kelly was awake.

He blinked a few times and felt her moving beside him.

"You okay?" he asked, wondering if the hours that had passed had changed her mind, made her pull away from him.

"Yeah. What about you?"

"I'm good." He wished he could see her face more clearly, but it was too dark in the room.

She hesitated for a minute before she finally asked, "Are you sure this is going to work out?"

"Why wouldn't it?"

"I don't know. It scares me when things change. I just... don't want to lose you."

"You're not going to lose me, Kelly. I'll never let that happen."

"Okay."

She sounded so small and worried that he pulled her into his arms, and he let out a sigh of relief when she wrapped her arms around in him response.

He found her lips in the dark and kissed her until she was soft and eager against him. Whatever her worries—and those were natural and expected—she obviously still wanted him as much as she had that evening.

Peter's body was responding to her as helplessly as it always did, and soon he was hard, hot, breathless.

"Again?" Kelly asked.

"Why not?"

"No reason, I guess. But I'm a little sore from before, so you'll have to be gentle."

He rolled her over onto her back and moved over her, thrilled and amazed that he was finally able to do it after wanting it for so long. He murmured, "I can be as gentle as you want."

~

Peter was almost high on the excitement of the change in their relationship for most of the day—until they got back to Savannah.

Kelly had been soft and sweet the whole time, letting him kiss her, giving him slanting little looks, but her manner changed as soon as they walked into the old Beaufort house and she greeted her grandmother.

Mrs. Beaufort gave him a sharp look as if she suspected he'd been up to no good, but she didn't say much. Fortunately it was already after dinnertime, so they didn't have to spend much time making small talk.

But Peter knew something had changed, and his heart sank as he kept searching Kelly's face.

She was going to pull away from him, now that she'd come home, now that she was back to her normal self.

He told himself not to overreact. It was to be expected. Coming back from a trip often felt like a letdown. It didn't mean she didn't want him anymore.

They went through their normal evening rituals, and Kelly was reading in bed when Peter came out of the bathroom after taking his shower.

He got into bed beside her, rolling on his side so he was facing her.

"What?" Kelly asked, her eyes still on her textbook.

"I didn't say anything."

She turned her head toward him. "But I could feel you thinking."

"And what was I thinking?" He tried to sound light and teasing, but he wasn't sure he was very successful.

Kelly sighed and lowered her book. "Peter, it's just too weird for me to have sex here, with my grandmother just upstairs."

Okay. That was clear enough.

He tried not to convey his disappointment. "She wouldn't hear anything."

"I know. It's just the idea of it. I'm sorry."

"You don't have to be sorry. We agreed we'd just play it by ear, and we're definitely not going to have sex if you don't want to."

"I don't want you to be upset." She was eying him worriedly.

He obviously needed to work more on his expression. He smiled at her. "I'm not upset."

"Yes, you are. You always get all bland and nonchalant when you're upset. You think I don't know you?"

He relaxed against his pillow, a fond resignation washing over him. Of course she knew him. Better than anyone else. "Okay. I'm a little disappointed since I was hoping to keep having sex with you. But I get it. There's no pressure. I mean it."

She nodded. "Thanks." She scooted over toward him and wrapped an arm around his chest. "I can feel Grandmama up there, shaking her head in disapproval."

Peter could almost feel her too. "But I don't get why she'd be disapproving. We're married. Surely she's not against sex between married people."

"I don't know. There's no telling. But she's definitely disapproving."

"She doesn't seem to like me."

"She doesn't like anyone."

"But she was all excited about your sisters getting married. I don't get why she doesn't think I'm a good option. I'm a decent guy, and I'm a Blake. I would have thought that would mean something to her."

"Yeah," Kelly admitted, idly stroking his chest. "I would have thought so too. I don't know. I think she never expected me to get married at all. I'm the one who stays home."

"That's not fair to you."

"It's not about being fair. It's about who she's always thought I was."

"But who she always thought you were isn't really who you are. You can't let that shape the course of your life."

"I know. I'm not."

He couldn't help but wonder if that was actually true.

He suddenly realized he was never going to win Kelly's heart until he could first win her grandmother's approval. At the moment it seemed like an impossible task.

He cleared his throat. "If you have any advice for getting your grandmother to like me, I'd be very glad to hear it."

"Seriously?" She lifted her head to look down at him.

"Yeah. What should I do?"

"I don't really know. Maybe you could ask her about the family and about the house and her treasures and the Pride and everything. She loves to talk about all that, and she loves when people are interested. But you'll have to be convincing. She knows when people are faking."

"Okay. I'll do my best."

"It's not a big deal," Kelly said. "I mean, you don't have to turn yourself inside out for her. She's stubborn and strange and hard to get along with. We're only going to be married for five more weeks, so it's probably not worth the effort."

"It's worth it. I'll do my best."

He wasn't sure exactly what Kelly thought about his declaration, but she stayed snuggled up against him as she relaxed into sleep.

He stayed awake for a long time, holding her and thinking. Wondering if Kelly could ever get to the point of loving him enough to leave her grandmother.

# EIGHT

On Saturday Kelly stood in front of the mirror, wondering if the woman in the reflection was really her.

They were getting ready for the fancy wedding reception that her grandmother had planned with Mrs. Blake for her and Peter, and her grandmother had insisted she wear something that looked like a wedding dress.

So she'd gone out shopping with Rose and Deanna a few days ago, and they'd bought the dress she wore right now. It was sleek and fitted in white silk, with beautiful embroidery and beading at the neckline and at the waist. It could have been a wedding dress. Or a cocktail dress. Either way, it wasn't anything that Kelly normally wore.

She'd already done her makeup, and her hair was loose as she decided what to do with it. She couldn't help but recognize how pretty she looked—and nothing like her regular self at all.

The week had gone quickly as she and Peter had fallen back into their regular class and work schedule. He hadn't brought up sex again, which was both a relief and a disappointment. She kept remembering what the weekend away had felt like with him, but it now seemed more like a pleasant fantasy. Not like something that was part of her real life.

Besides, she needed to be careful, or she'd never be satisfied with her normal life when they both went their own ways again.

Peter had been taking a shower, but he came out now, wearing just his underwear.

She vigilantly kept her eyes up on his face.

He stopped when he saw her, so abruptly it confused her.

"What?" she asked, turning around to face him.

He blinked a few times, his eyes running up and down her body in a way she couldn't possibly misinterpret. "You look gorgeous."

"Thanks." She was smiling as she turned back to face the mirror, reminding herself not to sneak a peek at Peter's body in the reflection.

"Are you going to keep your hair like that?"

She shrugged. "I don't know."

"Braids might look a little strange with the dress."

Of course they would. She'd gone back to wearing her braids since they made her feel more like herself, but she no longer really liked how she looked in them. She definitely shouldn't wear them to the reception. "Yeah. I know."

Peter walked over until he was standing directly behind her, looking at her through the mirror. His face was sober as he wrapped one arm around her, pulling her back against him. "What are you afraid of, Kelly?"

She couldn't look away from his eyes, although she was strangely bewildered by the sight of them together, him mostly naked, her in this dress. "I don't know. It felt different when we were in Vegas, or when we were on our honeymoon. I could be someone different there. But I'm not sure... I'm not sure I can be someone different here."

"You can. You can if you want to be."

"I don't know what I want." She felt almost helpless as she admitted the truth to him.

He nodded, his eyes still holding hers with that same sober intensity. "I know you don't."

Neither of them spoke for a long moment as they gazed at themselves together in the mirror. Then Kelly finally cleared her throat and pulled away from him gently. "You better get dressed. We don't want to be late."

"I know," he said with a sigh, releasing her and walking over to where he'd laid out a black suit. "I'm already making little enough progress with your grandmother. She'd never forgive me if I made us late to this party."

He'd evidently been serious about trying to get her grandmother to like him. All week he'd been meticulously polite, asking about the Beaufort history and all the collectibles she'd filled this house with and even asking about the names of the Pride. Grandmama's manner hadn't changed with him though.

Peter was right. For some reason, she didn't like him—her disapproval stronger toward him than toward almost anyone else in their social circle.

It didn't make any sense. Peter had never been a prude, but he was thoroughly decent—kind and intelligent and gentle at his heart. He was much more of a gentleman than Mitchell had been when Deanna had married him, and Grandmama had been so absolutely set on that marriage.

Kelly just couldn't understand it. She wanted everyone to love Peter as much as she did.

She pulled the top part of her hair back with a silver clip and studied the result in the mirror. It looked really nice, so she left it that way.

Her ring had slipped down as she'd done her hair, so she slid it back up on her ring finger. "Everyone keeps asking when you're going to get this ring resized for me," she said, trying to get them back into normal conversation.

Peter had been pulling up his pants, but he glanced over at her words. "Oh, yeah. I really should get it resized for you soon."

"It's probably not worth it. In another four weeks you'll be getting it back, so you'd have to get it resized again."

Something flickered on his face, so briefly she barely registered it. "Yeah, but people will think it's strange if I let you go around wearing a ring that's way too big for you."

"I guess." She gazed down at the big ring. She liked the look of it now—far more than she would have liked a regular wedding band and diamond engagement ring. The signet ring had the Blake crest on it. It felt like it was really a part of Peter. He'd given her something that was truly his. "Although it's better than the cheap ring you have to wear."

"I like the cheap ring," he said with a smile, turning his wedding band on his finger.

"Don't you dare say it reminds you of me."

He chuckled. "I won't, although it does. Not because it's cheap though."

She wasn't really sure what he meant by that, and she was too nervous to pursue it. She watched as he pulled on his shirt and buttoned it. He was still looking down with a smile on his face as if he was thinking of something that made him happy.

She wondered what it was.

~

Two hours later Peter was trying to hold back a wave of pleased possessiveness as he and Kelly circulated through the large ornate ballroom, which was full of well-dressed people chatting and drinking champagne.

There would be some formal toasts later, but most of the party was simply going to be this kind of mingling. Peter was relieved. At least this way he and Kelly could have a little freedom and not be trapped at a table for hours.

He wondered if it was normal to be this proud of one's wife. She was beautiful and smart and funny and generous and sexy and generally amazing, and she was here on his arm, wearing his ring, with all these people to witness the fact that she was his wife.

No amount of mental lecturing could bring him back down to earth. Maybe it was partly the champagne.

They were talking to his mother, who was looking happier than he could remember seeing her. That was another reason for him to feel good. He'd disappointed her in a lot of ways, but at least she was pleased by this, by Kelly.

Of course, she assumed it was a marriage that would last, but Peter hadn't yet given up his hope of that happening. Kelly had pulled away after their honeymoon, but she wasn't completely settled in that. He saw her watching him sometimes. He was pretty sure she still wanted him.

Kelly wasn't the kind of person who liked things to change. She'd been upset when her sisters had married, although she'd refused to admit it to him. She liked the security of her world as it had always been. But he was hopeful that she would slowly see the benefit of allowing their relationship to keep changing. He just needed to make her feel safe enough to let go again, even here in Savannah.

When they moved on from his mother, Peter saw that Kelly's face was slightly strained.

"What is it?" he murmured, easing her aside before they could be greeted by anyone else.

She shook her head and smiled. "Nothing."

"Don't lie to me. What's wrong? Was it something with my mother?"

"No, no. It's just that sometimes I feel kind of... kind of... guilty. Like we're lying to all these people who are here to celebrate our marriage."

His heart jumped painfully. "It isn't a lie. We really are married."

"I know. I know. But it's not what they're all thinking."

"Maybe not. But it doesn't matter what they're all thinking. It only matters what's right for us."

"Yeah. I guess so." Her eyes had moved so they were resting on her grandmother across the room, who was talking to that pompous ass named Morris Alfred Something-or-other III.

"Kelly—"

"I know," she interrupted, her face clearing back into a natural expression. "It's silly to feel guilty."

He knew she wasn't yet over her concerns, no matter how casual she was pretending to be. He cupped her face with one hand. "We can be anyone we want to be, Kelly."

She nodded, her eyes wide and open. "I know."

"Do you?"

"Yes. I didn't mean to mess up the party. We were having a good time."

They went back to mingling, but Peter didn't enjoy it as much as he had before. He kept reminding himself that they still had another month, and there was no reason to feel hopeless.

After another month, maybe she wouldn't be so eager to take off his ring.

~

Kelly needed a little break.

The party was better than she'd expected it to be, and she loved the way other women looked at Peter, like he was something impressive, a husband they'd like to have. But her feelings were in an uproar after the little conversation with Peter, and she needed to get some space to breathe and pull herself together.

So after another fifteen minutes, she said she had to go to the bathroom. After she had, she slipped into a small side room off the main ballroom so she could sit down and relax for a minute.

She was startled, after she sat down on an antique sofa, to discover she wasn't alone in the room.

The other person was a pretty blonde who was standing near the window. She looked elegant and expensive in a gown with a vintage-looking ivory top and a sleek black skirt, but her expression when she turned around wasn't cool or pretentious at all.

She gave Kelly a sincere, sunny smile. "Oh, hi. I didn't hear you come in." She spoke with a slight accent—maybe French.

"I'm sorry. I didn't think anyone was in here."

"Don't be sorry. I just had to get away from the ballroom for a while. There was beer, and I... I don't do well around beer."

Kelly frowned in concern. "Really? I'm sorry. Most people are drinking champagne, but I guess a few people wanted—"

"Oh, there's nothing to be sorry about. It's my issue, not yours. The smell of it makes me… panic. Just something from the past I can't seem to completely get over. My husband was going to see if he could take care of it, but if he can't, it's really no big deal." The other woman walked over and extended her hand. "I'm Etta."

"Kelly."

Etta gave her a playful smile as she sat down beside her. "I know who you are, of course. You're the new bride."

Kelly felt that sliver of guilt again. "Yeah. I'm sorry we haven't met before. The party is so big I don't know half the people here. My grandmother and Peter's mother invited everyone. Even some of the Damons are here if you can believe it."

Etta's eyes sparkled in a very appealing way. "Really? You know the Damons?"

"Only Benjamin and his mother. We grew up in the same neighborhood. My sister actually dated Ben in high school."

Benjamin was the nephew of Cyrus Damon, a billionaire with a corporate empire that stretched around the world, an army of old-fashioned hotels, clubs, restaurants, and tea houses, each held up the same standard of excellence. Cyrus also had three other nephews, although Kelly had never met them.

"I've met Ben's wife Mandy too, a few times. She's so sweet. And Harrison really helped my sister out before she got married," Kelly continued since Etta seemed interested. "It was because Ben asked him to help, but I know she really appreciated it. She said he was a great guy. Deanna said he and his wife were supposed to be here tonight, but I haven't seen them yet."

"I'm sure they're around somewhere. So, if this is your celebration, why are you hiding in this room with me?"

"I'm not hiding," Kelly said, surprised by the other woman's bluntness but kind of liking it just the same. "I just needed a little break. It's... it's overwhelming."

"The party or the marriage?"

Kelly gave a little shrug. "Both, I guess."

"I haven't met your husband yet, but I've got a pretty good intuition about people. I can tell just from looking at him that he's got a really good heart."

"He does." Kelly felt a warmth spread out from her heart.

"And he's obviously crazy in love with you," Etta added.

Kelly's cheeks grew hot, and she started to argue with this statement before she caught herself. She could hardly go around at their wedding celebration and declare that her new husband wasn't in love with her.

If Etta saw her embarrassment, she didn't say anything. "What is he like?"

"Oh, he's great," Kelly replied, relieved by something easy to talk about. "He's really smart and funny. He started college late because he went to travel around the world for a few years. He's been everywhere. His family has a lot of money, but he won't take any of it. He's determined to do everything on his own merit."

"That's definitely unusual. What does he want to do?"

"He's in hotel management. He wants to buy a property and turn it into a hotel or bed and breakfast. He's been working like crazy and saving up for years so he can make a down payment after he graduates."

"Well, your brother-in-law does hotels, right? He could help."

"He could, but Peter won't take that kind of help. He'd feel like he hadn't earned it."

"So he doesn't want any investors at all? It's pretty hard to run a business like that without accepting any financial help."

"I know. He knows that too. I think he'd accept investors if it was really a business arrangement. He just doesn't want help from his family or people he feels might be obligated to help him out. Don't ask me to explain it, but he's really serious about it. He only wants to succeed on his own merits." Kelly sighed, thinking wistfully of Eden Manor and how perfect it had been for Peter. "We actually found a house that would make the best bed and breakfast, up in North Georgia. But he doesn't think he can afford it, and he won't let his parents or my brothers-in-law help him out with it."

"Oh." Etta looked thoughtful. "Maybe he can find another investor, one he wouldn't feel was obligated."

"Maybe. I hope so. He's worked so hard, and I know he could make a success of it." Kelly suddenly realized how much she'd been talking to this stranger. "Sorry. I didn't mean to ramble on about him."

"That's okay," Etta said with a knowing look. "I think it's a pretty common thing to do about a new husband."

Kelly was trying to think of something to say in response, when a very handsome man came striding into the room without warning. He was tall and fit with dark hair and lovely chocolate brown eyes. Although she'd never met him, Kelly recognized him immediately.

Harrison Damon. As if their conversation earlier had summoned him.

"Are you all right, sweetheart?" he asked, his eyes on Etta. "They've put the beer away, so I think it's okay for you to come out."

Kelly jerked in surprised and turned to look at the other woman.

Etta gave her a look of guilty amusement. "I'm sorry. I was very bad."

Kelly looked from Etta to Harrison, who had sat down beside her and reached for her hand. They were obviously married. "Why didn't you tell me?"

"I should have. I know. But it's sometimes strange to go around announcing to the world that you're married to a Damon."

Harrison was smiling, although he looked slightly confused. "Were you pretending not to be trapped in this unfortunate marriage with me?"

"Yes. And she was talking about how great a guy you are and everything."

He turned his eyes to Kelly and reached out a hand with a cultured civility that made her feel very special. "I'm sorry I didn't introduce myself before. I'm Harrison Damon. We haven't met, have we?"

"No, we haven't," she said, shaking his hand. "But you really helped out Deanna with that contract. She still talks about it."

Before she'd married Mitchell, Deanna had called in a favor with Benjamin Damon, and Harrison had come to Savannah to help negotiate the marriage contract. Back then, the Beauforts hadn't been able to afford a few hours of a lawyer's time.

A lot had changed since then. Occasionally Kelly still missed the old days of her and her sisters working together to make it in the world.

Harrison smiled as if enlightened. "That was great fun. I can't remember another contract I had such a good time negotiating." He glanced back at the door into the ballroom. "Marriage has definitely improved her husband. I was just talking to him. I also met your husband. He helped me out with the beer. I was very impressed with him."

Kelly somehow knew that Harrison didn't give that kind of praise lightly, and she bloomed at the compliment, as much as if it had been given to her. "He really is great."

"And did he tell you that he was going into the hotel business?" Etta asked.

"Is he?"

"Yes," Etta said before Kelly could reply. "He's got a property in mind. He's just looking for an investor."

"Really." Harrison's eyes moved between his wife and Kelly's face. Then he reached into his jacket pocket and pulled out a business card. "Tell him to call me."

Kelly stared down at the card, flustered and excited both. "Thank you. I will. That's so nice. I don't know that he'd want it to be a Damon place, but—"

"Oh, I know. I wasn't thinking of bringing it into the Damon fold. I do a few things on my own, you know." He twitched his eyebrows at her, making the words teasing rather than reproachful. "I wouldn't mind talking to him though. He really impressed me."

Kelly was almost hugging herself with excitement as she closed her fingers around the business card. She could hardly wait to see Peter so she could tell him.

Etta gave her a little smile, like they shared a secret. "He only says that when someone reminds him of himself."

"Hey!" Harrison objected, as his wife and Kelly both laughed.

# NINE

"What do you mean you told him about Eden Manor?" Peter asked, his voice low, but his face tightening into a frown.

Kelly had been so excited about her conversation with Harrison Damon that she'd started telling Peter the story as they were walking to their car after the party. Since several other people were making the same walk—including her sisters and grandmother—she'd told him discreetly so no one else could hear what she was saying.

"I was just talking," she explained, realizing Peter must have misunderstood and thought she'd made a point of going around and asking for money from any stray rich person she saw. "Not even to him. I was talking to his wife, only I didn't know who she was, and she was asking about you, so I just mentioned it. Then she told Harrison, and he gave me his card to give to you. I think he was serious about possibly investing. It's amazing, really."

Peter had his hand on her back as they walked, but it didn't feel affectionate as much as him keeping her close so they could continue their low-voiced conversation. "I don't want to run a Damon property."

"I know that." She was starting to get annoyed that he was acting so displeased with such a great opportunity. "He knows that too. I told him. He said he does some things on his own. He'd just be a silent partner or something. Why are you acting so grumpy about it?"

They'd reached the car, and they both stopped, facing each other. "You know I want to do this on my own. I don't need you going around soliciting donations for me."

She sucked in a breath, feeling like she'd just been slapped. She was about to snap out a response when she saw her grandmother approaching. Instead, she slipped the business card into Peter's pocket and whispered quickly, "Fine. Whatever. He told me to give you his card so I did. You can take it or leave it. I'll know better than to try to support you again." Her voice cracked on the last words, something she hated. She wasn't an emotional person by nature. She didn't know why being married to Peter was taking such a toll on her mental stability.

When Peter opened his mouth to reply, she turned away from him intentionally. "Let me open the door for you, Grandmama," she said with false cheerfulness.

Her grandmother was shooting suspicious looks at Peter, as if she somehow knew he'd upset Kelly. "If your husband was a gentleman, he'd open the door himself."

This wasn't fair. At all. Peter always went out of his way to open doors—not just for Grandmama but for Kelly too. His face twisted slightly, as if he was having to restrain himself from replying.

Even though she was exasperated with him herself, she couldn't help but defend him. "Don't be snippy, Grandmama. You know Peter is always doing things for you. He sometimes lets me open my own doors because he knows I'm not helpless."

Her grandmother tsked her tongue but didn't respond, which was a relief. Kelly helped her into the front seat while Peter got into the driver's seat. When Kelly had climbed in the back, she saw Peter giving her a questioning look in the rearview mirror.

She shook her head briefly to indicate that the rest of the conversation would have to wait until they were alone. They drove home in silence, but Peter kept watching her through the mirror. It made Kelly very self-conscious, especially since she couldn't seem to control her emotions.

It shouldn't have hurt so much—Peter throwing her gesture of genuine support back in her face. She knew he was irrationally stubborn about accepting help.

But how could she be his wife, or even his friend, if he refused to let her help him at all?

It was only a fifteen-minute drive home, but it seemed to last forever. When they finally pulled into the driveway, Kelly was exhausted and drained from trying to keep a natural expression on her face.

She just wanted to go to bed. Except Peter would be right there in bed beside her.

They walked with her grandmother into the house, and Peter set down the flowers she'd brought back with her. Kelly was about to head to her room to change clothes when Peter reached out for her hand. "Do you want to take a walk?" he asked softly.

She understood the request and the significant look he gave her. He wanted to talk, to continue the conversation they'd barely started before. Kelly would prefer to put it off since the discussion promised to be hard and she was already exhausted, but she couldn't bring herself to push Peter away.

She stretched her arm out until he'd wrapped his hand around hers. "Okay. Do you need anything before we go, Grandmama? I'll put the flowers up when I get back."

"I suppose that's acceptable," her grandmother said in her typical imperious manner. She aimed a cool look at Peter. "Don't keep her out too late or take her to a dangerous part of town."

Peter visibly bit back a response, turning his face away to hide his expression.

"Grandmama, please," Kelly sighed. She just couldn't understand why her grandmother treated Peter this way. He'd done absolutely nothing to deserve it. "Don't be that way."

"And why shouldn't I be concerned about my granddaughter? You're the only one I have left."

For some reason the last words sent a shooting pain through Kelly's chest. She almost strangled on a sudden rise of emotion as she processed the sentiment.

Her grandmother had three granddaughters, but two of them had already married and moved away. Kelly hadn't. Kelly wasn't supposed to. Kelly was all her grandmother had left.

"Let's go," Peter murmured, pulling Kelly toward him.

She nodded and waved good-bye to her grandmother since she couldn't bring herself to speak. She let Peter lead her down the front steps and the paved front walk until they reached the sidewalk. They'd moved out of sight of the house before Peter said, his voice rough and tense, "Don't let her manipulate you that way."

"She's not manip—"

"Of course she is." He sounded angry—angrier than the situation warranted. "She's trying to make you feel guilty so you won't leave her to live your own life. And it's not right. I know you love her, Kelly, but it's not right."

"It's just her way. She doesn't mean any harm."

"I'm sure she doesn't mean any harm, but she's going to do harm anyway if you let her push you around that way."

"I don't let her push me around. I've always stood up to her." Kelly's shoulders stiffened in automatic defensiveness. "You know I have. She's not usually this bad. I don't know what's gotten into her lately, but I'm sure it's just a passing thing."

"It's not a passing thing. She doesn't like me, and she's trying to get you to dump me. She's going to keep doing it until she wins."

Kelly felt more and more like crying, a fact she found infuriating. There was nothing to cry about here. "It's not about you. It can't be. We've been friends for years, and she's always been perfectly happy for me to hang out with you."

"But she's never been threatened by me before. Now we're married, and she's afraid there's a real possibility of me taking you away from her. You know it as well as I do. That's the only explanation for her behavior." He was clearly stewing about the situation, his muscles tense, his jaw clenched, his skin damp with perspiration, although it wasn't a particularly warm evening.

"But you're *not* going to take me away from her."

Peter flinched. And his tone was different as he muttered, "She doesn't know that."

Her grandmother thought the marriage was real. And the fact that it wasn't—that it had always only been an accident—was inexplicably painful to Kelly. Peter was still holding her right hand, but she fiddled with his signet ring on her left hand.

Pretty soon she would have to take it off.

She should probably just go ahead and take it off now since everything was getting so complicated.

She didn't want to take the ring off though. She loved it.

They walked in silence for another minute until they reached a small park, where Peter led her over to a bench. It was late, and the only people around were a few other couples walking and a homeless man on the sidewalk across the street.

Kelly sat on the bench, still holding Peter's hand, and tried to get her emotions under control, the way she'd always lived her life before.

"I'm sorry about before," Peter said without transition.

"Sorry about what?"

"About before. About Damon. I'm sorry I reacted the way I did."

The apology should have made her feel better, but it just made a shudder intensify inside her, like something strong was growing, desperately trying to get out. She swallowed hard, staring in front of her, at a small fountain, rather than at Peter's face. "Why did you?"

"I don't know. It was wrong. I know you were just trying to help."

She turned to look at him, recognizing some sort of emotional struggle in his expression. "I can understand not wanting to rely on your parents or take money from Mitchell, but why won't you even let *me* help you."

He cleared his throat. "I want you to help me. I do."

"And yet you acted like I was sneaking around, turning you into a charity case."

"I didn't mean that."

"I thought you trusted me more than that."

"I do trust you." His voice became more urgent, and he turned to face her. "Kelly, you know I trust you. I just spent so many years of my life with people assuming I could never do anything on my own, that the only reason I accomplished anything was because I was a Blake. It's hard... it's hard to get over that, even though I know I should."

She was so restless that she slid her fingers in his grip, not trying to pull away, just needing to move. "When people love you, they want to help. It doesn't mean they think you can't do things on your own."

His eyes shot quickly to her face.

Since she was on a roll, she went on, "If there's something I can do that will help or support you, then I'm going to do it. I hope you'll... you'll let me."

"Kelly," he said huskily, raising his free hand to brush a strand of hair back from her face. "I want that. I really do."

Her breathing accelerated. "Do you? Even if it means relying on someone else occasionally?"

He leaned forward, his eyes hot and tender and fierce all at once. "If it means relying on you."

She was still trying to process the words when he closed his mouth over hers, claiming her lips in a soft, deep kiss. She responded to him as instinctively as she always did, reaching up to tangle her fingers in his hair and easing her body closer to his.

The kiss went on longer than it should have—on a bench in the middle of a public park. Soon Kelly's heart and head and body were all throbbing with her need for Peter.

"Can we go home?" he asked hoarsely, pulling his lips away from her just long enough to speak. "Or somewhere else? I don't care where we go, baby, but we have to go somewhere, or else I'll have to just take you right here in the park."

She choked on amusement and desire both, clutching at the lapels to his jacket. "Home is the closest. But when did you get to be such an alpha male?"

"I don't know. It must come from being married to you." He'd been pressing more kisses against her mouth and skin, but he finally pulled away with a groan and stood up. He reached a hand down toward her, pulling her up beside him. "Let's go."

They walked the two blocks back to the old house quickly, but instead of leading her in the front door, Peter walked her around the house to the summer house in the back garden. "We'll have more privacy here," he murmured, pulling her inside with him and closing the door.

Before she could question this choice—since she'd never imagined having sex in the summer house in her own backyard—Peter pushed her back against the wall and kissed her again.

All of her other thoughts scattered when she felt his lips on her again, his hot, hard body pressed snugly against hers. She twined her arms around him and fisted her hands in the back of his jacket, moaning low in her throat as pleasure and excitement rose together inside her.

They kissed until they were both aroused. He was pushing his groin into her belly, letting her feel how hard he was, and she'd raised one of her legs to wrap it around his thighs. Kelly felt wild and a little sleazy, making love to him like this in the summer house, but there was no way she wanted to stop.

No one was around. No one but her and Peter.

They were rocking together against the wall, mimicking the motion of sex, until Kelly's body throbbed so intensely she couldn't keep quiet.

"Please," she begged, clutching at his back. "Please, Peter, now."

He groaned and started to push up her skirt as she fumbled to unfasten his pants. "Condom," he gasped when she'd pulled his erection out from his underwear.

"In my purse."

Her clutch was looped on her wrist, and she let Peter open it, find the condom she'd stuck in on a whim, and unwrap it. He rolled it on and then parted her legs, lifting one of her thighs so he could position himself at her entrance.

Then he was pushing inside.

She cried out softly, helplessly, at the feel of him inside her. It took a little adjusting for them to get into a position where he could thrust, but even the shifts and maneuvers sent tingling pleasure through her body.

Then he was kissing her again, pumping his hips against her as she kept one leg wrapped around him tightly. She was off-balance, so she held on tight, and the precarious position just made the whole thing hotter.

Peter was grunting out, "Kelly" and "Yes," as he built up his rhythm, and Kelly's vision blurred as she tightened herself around him. Everything feel so good, so deep, so intense that she thought she might actually black out.

It wasn't long before she was coming, biting her lip to muffle her cry of release. Then Peter was coming too, moaning helplessly against her mouth as his body jerked and shuddered.

They were both panting as he pulled out of her, and she was finally able to lower her leg. Her knees buckled, and she almost slid to the floor as she pushed down her skirt and tried to pull herself together.

When Peter had taken care of the condom and pulled up his pants, he took her in his arms, holding her tightly, burying his face in the crook of her neck.

Neither one of them spoke. They just held each other. And Kelly had never felt so known, so cared for, so protected in her life.

He wasn't just her friend. He was her husband. And she wanted both of those things to be true.

To remain.

"I guess that's what a regular guy does when he morphs into an alpha male," Kelly said, a lilt in her voice as she tried to find her normal manner again.

Peter chuckled and lifted his head so he could kiss her very gently. "I guess so."

"Let's go back in if that's okay. I think I need to lie down."

"Me too."

They were both laughing softly and holding hands as they discreetly entered the house. If her grandmother was still up, she wasn't anywhere in sight as they went down the hall toward their room.

Kelly was thinking that they still had a month left of this marriage, and she was going to enjoy it as much as she could. Because afterward, her life would return to the familiar one she'd always had, where things like this never happened.

～

Twenty minutes later, Peter stepped out of the shower, feeling exhausted and sated and embarrassingly thrilled.

He hadn't started the evening thinking they'd have sex at the end of it, but Kelly had obviously been as overwhelmed and needy as he'd been.

Things were going well. Better than he could have expected.

Kelly wasn't in the bedroom when he walked out. He had no idea where she was. So even though he just wore his pajama pants, he opened the bedroom door and took a few steps down the hall.

He heard voices from the parlor.

It was late. Almost one in the morning. Her grandmother shouldn't still be up, but evidently she was.

"I hope you remember who you are." That was Mrs. Beaufort. The voice was unmistakable.

"What is that supposed to mean?" Kelly asked rather sharply.

Curious and a little worried by Kelly's tone, Peter walked a few steps closer to the opened door of the parlor.

"It means you're a Beaufort, and I expect you to act accordingly."

"I'm actually a Blake. I'm married, remember."

Peter's breath hitched. He couldn't believe she'd actually said that.

"As if I could forget. But I have no concerns about the marriage lasting for very long. You'll always be a Beaufort."

"What do you mean the marriage won't last long? Why wouldn't it last long?"

"That boy is not an appropriate match for you."

"He's not a boy. He's a man. It's not right for you to treat him so badly."

Peter had tensed at Mrs. Beaufort's insulting comments about him, but his heart was racing wildly as he registered Kelly's responses.

"When have I treated him badly?"

"You always treat him badly. You act like he's nothing. But he isn't nothing. He's my husband. And there's no reason for you to assume he's not going to stay that way."

"You will come to your senses soon."

"Stop it." Kelly was angry now. It was evident from her voice. "Just stop it. We've tried to be patient since I know this was sudden, but I'm really tired of you talking about him that way. He's amazing. He's the best guy ever. He doesn't deserve for you to treat him like that."

"I treat people in the way I feel most appropriate. You know that. Why should I change now?"

"Because you're supposed to love me. And if you love me, then you'll accept that I love him."

Peter flattened his hand against the wall, hardly believing what he was hearing.

"Don't be foolish," Mrs. Beaufort said from inside the room.

"I'm not foolish. I've known Peter for a long time. I know him better than anyone. I'm not some little girl who isn't thinking clearly. He's my husband, and I love him, and I don't want you to treat him so badly anymore.

"He's not family."

"I know he's not family, but that doesn't change anything. Why are you so set against him?"

There was a long silence before Kelly's grandmother finally replied, "I have my ways."

"Well, your ways need to change a little. Please, Grandmama. If you love me."

Peter couldn't see either of their expressions, but it felt like something had happened between them in the room.

Then Mrs. Beaufort said in her normal cool tone. "You look a little feverish, dear. I think you should go lie down. Get that husband of yours to get a cool cloth for your face."

It sounded like Kelly laughed. "I will. Goodnight."

She left the parlor before Peter could react, and she pulled to a stop when she saw him there.

He stared at her, wondering if he'd just imagined the conversation he'd heard.

She was taking his side—against her grandmother. It was like some sort of miracle had happened.

He opened his mouth to say something, but she raised a finger to her lips to keep him quiet. Then she took his hand as they walked back to their bedroom.

Peter wanted to say something as she closed the door. He wanted to say everything. But he wasn't capable of speaking at the moment.

So he pulled Kelly into a hug.

She returned the embrace, burying her face against his shoulder for a minute. When she lifted her head, she was smiling. "You shouldn't eavesdrop, you know."

He couldn't help but chuckle. "Just don't tell your grandma."

# TEN

A week later, Kelly stretched out on a chaise by the pool at James and Rose's house, where the family was gathered for the afternoon and a cookout. It was too early in the spring for Kelly to want to lie around in a bathing suit, so she was wearing a knit sundress over her suit. But she was still enjoying the mild air and sunshine.

Rose had just settled herself in the chaise beside her, which was no small feat since Rose was now almost seven months pregnant.

"You may have to rent a crane to get me up," Rose groaned, rubbing her rounded belly.

Kelly laughed. "I'm sure we can manage. Among us there are at least five able-bodied persons, and we'll have the two girls and Grandmama to supervise the lift."

"Thanks a lot."

Kelly's eyes were focused on the activity in the pool. Julie and Jill, Rose's stepdaughters, were playing Marco Polo with their father, James, and Peter. They were evidently all having a great time if the screams, laughter, and splashing were any evidence.

Peter was grinning widely as he launched a mock-escape from Julie, who was flailing toward him with her eyes tightly shut, screaming "Marco!" over and over again at the top of her lungs. Peter could easily have ducked under the water and swum past her without getting tagged, but he let her catch him instead, sending her into ecstatic squeals of victory.

Rose chuckled, her eyes fond as she watched the little girl. She'd been the girls' nanny before she became their stepmother, and she loved them as much as if they were her own.

They were her own in every way that mattered.

Kelly felt the strangest surge of envy as she saw her sister's expression. She wondered what it would be like to feel that way toward a child. She wondered if she would ever know. She'd never been particularly interested in kids, and she'd thought it a good possibility that she might never have them. So she wasn't quite sure where the feeling came from.

Rose glanced back over and caught her looking. "Peter is great with kids, isn't he?"

"Yeah." Kelly turned her eyes back to her husband. He was now hamming it up, moaning out "Marco," and making wild swings toward the others who responded, "Polo," in a way that guaranteed he'd never reach them. Both girls were giggling like crazy at his dramatics, easily revealing their location if Peter had seriously been trying to catch them.

"I'm sure Jill, Julie, and this one would love a couple of cousins," Rose teased, patting her stomach.

Kelly blinked. "Oh. No. No! I don't think so."

Rose looked a little surprised at the vehemence, but she didn't call her out on it. "I guess it's kind of early to be thinking in that direction yet. I mean, you haven't even graduated from college."

That was true, but it wasn't the issue. Not at all.

Ridiculously, it felt like a loss—that Kelly couldn't have a baby with Peter. She didn't even want to have kids anytime soon, but the knowledge that it would never happen felt like a loss just the same.

"What's the matter?" Rose asked, lifting her head to peer at Kelly in concern. "Did I say something stupid?"

"No. Of course not. It's nothing." Kelly smiled, brushing the poignancy away.

Rose obviously didn't believe her. "Is everything all right between you and Peter?"

"Sure. Why wouldn't it be?" Kelly didn't like lying to her sisters. She almost never did. But she and Peter had agreed to act like theirs was a real marriage, and she wasn't going to break her word to him.

"I don't know. It just looked like something was wrong. There are always ups and downs. James and I are crazy about each other, but we still argue over stupid things. Last night it was about him not rinsing out the sink after he spits his toothpaste."

"Oh, no. I'm with you on that one. I'd get so annoyed about all the dried gunk leftover."

"That's what I say! He says sometimes he's in a hurry, and it's no big deal since we each have our own sinks. But I still have to see it all over his sink! So Peter rinses out the sink?"

Kelly had never thought about it before. Just one more thing to love about Peter. "Yeah. Yeah, he does."

"He sounds like a keeper." Rose was smiling, her eyes on James, who was swinging Jill around in the pool playfully, after having caught her. "Anyway, my point was that no marriage is smooth sailing all the way."

"I know it's not."

"But you still look like something is wrong."

"Nothing is wrong." Kelly really wished Rose would drop the subject. Afraid she was going to spill everything if the interrogation continued, she searched her mind for something true that would also be not quite the core of the problem. When her eyes landed on her grandmother, who was across the pool deck fixing a pasta salad with Deanna, she thought of a perfect excuse. "Although Grandmama still doesn't like him. It's really obvious, and it makes it difficult for both me and Peter."

"That doesn't make any sense. I thought she'd be thrilled about him being a Blake. I mean, she planned that big party—"

"Yeah, she was happy about the party, but she's not happy about Peter. It doesn't seem to matter that he's a Blake. She just doesn't want me to be married to him."

Rose's lips turned down thoughtfully. "You know how she is. Maybe she's just giving him a hard time."

"I thought so at first, but she doesn't change, even when I called her on it and asked her not to do it. She doesn't want me to be married to him."

"But you *are* married to him. You've got to do what's best for you and Peter, even if she doesn't approve. You probably need to move out of the house pretty soon."

"Grandmama needs—"

"She needs someone with her, yes. But there are other options."

"I guess." Kelly sighed. She couldn't even imagine moving out of the house, leaving her grandmother alone. Especially not for a marriage that had an end date. She'd never let her world change that much. "We're not going to do anything until after graduation though."

"That makes sense. But just let me know if you need any alone time. I can always come over and stay with Grandmama for the evening while you and Peter get away."

For the past week since their walk after the party, Kelly and Peter had been finding alone time. Just this morning, when her grandmother had left to have brunch with a couple of friends at the country club, Peter had dragged Kelly into the bedroom and made love to her until she was limp and hoarse.

That night after the party last weekend, they'd somehow come to an unspoken understanding—that sex was a good possibility, as long as Grandmama wasn't in the house.

The game in the pool had evidently dissolved into a contest over who could make the biggest splash with a cannonball. All the votes were on James—since his daughters had full confidence in their daddy—but it was now Peter's opportunity to beat him.

Kelly gazed at Peter as he climbed out of the pool, water streaming down his lean, tanned body. He was gorgeous she realized with an unexpected pang of ownership. And he was so much more than just gorgeous.

"Deanna said you guys were thinking about buying a house up north for a bed and breakfast," Rose said, breaking into Kelly's thoughts.

Kelly gave a visible jerk. "Oh. Not really. I mean, Peter was kind of interested, but it was too expensive."

"I thought Deanna said that Harrison Damon had approached him about investing."

Kelly swallowed and glanced away from her sister. She hadn't known the news had gotten around. That would make Peter very unhappy. "He did. But I don't know if anything will come of that. Anyway, I can't—I mean, I don't want to leave Savannah."

"North Georgia isn't that far away."

"I know."

"It's not Grandmama, is it? Because you can't let her keep you from doing what you want to—"

"I'm not. It's not that. I just don't think it's the right thing for me."

"For you and Peter," Rose corrected.

Kelly was awash with guilt and confusion and frustration. "Right. For me and Peter. It doesn't feel quite right."

That wasn't true. The big house had felt exactly right for Peter. And if it hadn't meant Kelly would have to move so far away, she would have felt like it was exactly right for her too.

She and Peter had always talked about running a bed and breakfast or hotel together. They'd just been daydreams to Kelly though—not something that she could ever actually bring to fruition. Just the idea that other people took the idea seriously terrified her.

She didn't know why.

"Well, you never know. Maybe things will work out so it is the right thing. Or maybe there will be another, better opportunity."

"Maybe."

~

A couple of hours later, they'd all eaten burgers and hot dogs on the patio, and the group had dispersed again.

Rose had needed to rest, so she'd taken Jill and Julie inside to watch a movie with Grandmama. James was cleaning his grill, and Mitchell and Deanna were sitting nearby, chatting with him.

Peter and Kelly were stretched out on chaises on the far end of the pool deck, catching the last of the sun.

"You saw that I did the best cannonball, right?" Peter asked her, turning to gaze at her with a teasing grin. "Even the girls had to admit that I beat their daddy."

"Naturally. Everyone was suitably impressed."

"Are you included among those who were suitably impressed?"

She gave a huff of amusement. "Yes, I was absolutely blown away by the size of your splash. It was far bigger than any other man's splash. Probably the biggest and most impressive in the world."

Chuckling, he reached to take her hand in his. "Good. I'm glad you recognize that."

He didn't release her hand. Instead, he brought it over to rest on his thigh, and he stroked her palm gently with his thumb. He'd been touchy that way all week. She loved it. She wanted to touch him too.

But, more and more, all of his little touches were causing her stomach to churn with nervousness, even more than having sex with him did.

She didn't pull her hand away though. She knew it would hurt his feelings, and she wasn't willing to do that, no matter how confused and nervous she felt.

"Listen," Peter said after clearing his throat. "I wanted to tell you…"

Her heart jumped with a flare of urgency, like something important was about to happen. "Tell me what?"

"I… I called Harrison Damon yesterday."

She straightened up, pulling her hand back as she readjusted. "You did? I thought you weren't going to do it."

"I wasn't sure. But I've been thinking about it, and I realized you were right about me being so stubborn and not accepting help when it was offered. So I called him after all."

"Why didn't you tell me yesterday?" She was almost hurt that he'd done something so important without even mentioning it to her.

He shook his head and reached to take her hand again. "I don't know. I felt… weird about it. I wasn't even sure I was going to do it until I did."

"What did he say?"

"He's interested. He wants me to put together a business plan, which I'd have to do anyway."

"So you're really thinking about Eden Manor?"

"Yeah. It's perfect. It's exactly what we've always talked about."

She felt that surge of poignancy again—the one that was always fighting with her nerves. "Yeah. Yeah, it is. You should definitely do it."

She'd dropped her eyes, and he ducked his head down as if he was trying to see her expression. "I need to go back up there and get inside the house to make sure it's what we think it is and then see how much work needs doing. I called the seller's realtor, and she sounded excited to show it to me. I was thinking about going up tomorrow."

"That's good. That's a good idea. You don't want to wait too long."

He was still searching her face, like he was looking for something particular there—something she didn't understand. "If you were able to skip your class on Monday morning, you could come with me."

She blinked. "You want me to come?"

"Of course I want you to come. Why wouldn't I?"

"I don't know."

"So do you think you can come? You'd just have to miss the one class."

Kelly never skipped classes, but there was absolutely no reason why she couldn't this one time. The churning of her stomach was warning that it might be a mistake, but she wanted to go with Peter. She wanted to see Eden Manor again. She wanted to talk through plans with him. Even if she wouldn't be around to follow through with them.

"Yeah. Yeah, I can come."

Peter's whole body relaxed as he smiled and lifted her hand to kiss her knuckles. "Good."

~

The following afternoon Peter wiped a hand across his forehead and stared out at Eden Manor.

He was exhausted from a long day of traveling and then walking through the entire house, making notes and studying details. But his head was roaring with excitement, which was so much stronger than his fatigue.

This could happen. It could actually happen. It wouldn't be easy, but it was possible. He could own Eden Manor. He could turn it into a great bed and breakfast. He could do what he'd always wanted to do.

And Kelly might even do it with him.

The past week might have been the best week of his life, ever since he'd heard Kelly admit to her grandmother that she loved him, that she was on his side. He'd always known she loved him as a friend, but he was thinking it might be turning into more than that. He was almost convinced that she might stay married to him after graduation. She was here with him now. She seemed to love this house as much as he did.

He'd never really believed his dreams could come true, but it was starting to look like they might.

"So what do you think?" Kelly asked, coming up to stand beside him. She'd pulled her hair back in a ponytail, and she wore jeans and a fitted T-shirt that emphasized the slim lines of her gorgeous body.

Unable to resist the impulse, he wrapped one arm around her waist. "I love it."

"So do I," she admitted. "It's going to take a lot of work, but I'm sure it would be worth it. It's perfect."

The realtor's name was Missy, and she was young, tiny, and blond. She'd been locking up the doors to the house, but now she came out to join them.

"Now let me show you the garden," she said with a bright grin. "It's the most romantic thing you'll ever see.

Peter wondered how old she was. She looked about sixteen.

"I knew there would be a garden," Kelly said, smiling as if she were excited. "After all, the place is called Eden Manor."

Peter took her hand as they walked around the house. She never seemed to question why he did so. She must know how he felt about her, how close he wanted to be to her. She never pulled away. She must want it too.

She had to.

Behind the house were three outbuildings—a large shed, a run-down stable, and a guest house. Behind the outbuildings was a stone wall.

"It's a walled garden," Kelly gasped as she saw the locked door.

"Yes. It needs work, but it's so picturesque," Missy replied, still grinning in that infectious way. "It would be perfect for a B&B. Wait until you see."

She unlocked the door and gestured them inside.

The garden was completely overrun with weeds, and the bushes and tree branches were tangled into a mess. But

Peter could easily see how, with a lot of work, this garden could be one of the most appealing features of the entire property.

"Oh," Kelly breathed, clasping her hands together, "I love it!"

"It's just like *The Secret Garden*," Missy said from behind them. "I'm always thinking Mary and Colin and Dickon should sneak in and start fixing the place up."

Peter laughed, torn between studying the tangled foliage for what all needed doing and gazing at Kelly's awed face. "How long has it been since it's been worked on?"

"Years. The place has been unoccupied for ten years, ever since Mrs. Travis had to move into the nursing home. She always refused to sell it though, so it wasn't on the market until she died a few months ago. Her son doesn't have time or interest in fixing the place up, so he's just selling it as is."

"Okay," Peter said, realizing he better keep his cool and not let Missy see how excited he was about the place. After all, he'd need to negotiate a good price. "Thanks for showing us around. There's a lot of work to do, but it might have potential."

"My pleasure," Missy said, closing the garden door behind them as they left. "Just let me know if you have any questions or want to move forward on it."

After saying their good-byes and taking one last look at the house, Peter and Kelly got back into his car and stared at each other.

"So what do you think?" Kelly asked.

Peter had put the key in the ignition, but he hadn't turned it on. "I love it."

"I do too. I think you should do it."

He wished she would say "we" instead of "you." Surely she knew he wanted her to be part of the process. "Yeah. I think it's too good to pass up."

"So don't waste any time. Write up the business proposal and send it to Harrison. He's not going to agree to anything that's not excellent, so you'll know it's a good plan if he wants to invest."

"Yeah." He was staring out at the house, his head still spinning. He was overwhelmed with a sudden fear—at the knowledge that he was about to ask something that could decide his future—and he had trouble speaking through the tension in his throat. "What should I... What should I tell him about the... the management?"

"What do you mean?" Her eyes were wide, like she had no idea what he was talking about.

"Should I tell him it will be just me? Or should I plan on it being both of us?"

"Oh." She blinked a few times and then jerked her gaze away from his. "Oh."

He reached out to turn her face toward his. Since the question was out in the open now, he felt more confident, more certain, more sure that this was the right thing. "Kelly, you must know that I want us to stay together. I want us to do this together. You *must* know that."

She gave her head a little shake. "I didn't... I mean, I don't... You know I can't move here, Peter."

"Why not? Because of your grandmother?"

"Partly, but not just that. My whole life is in Savannah. My family."

"Why can't I become part of your family?" She looked genuinely torn, upset, which irrationally gave him hope. He knew she'd put up some resistance, but obviously part of her really wanted this, wanted to be with him for real.

"It's not that, Peter."

"Then what is it?" She'd turned away from him again, so he gently moved her face back so he could see her expression, so she would meet his eyes. "I know you love me, Kelly. You can't tell me that you don't."

"Of course I love you. I've always loved you."

"As more than just a friend."

"Obviously, I like having sex with you, but there's more than that to a marriage—if we were to make this a real marriage, I mean."

"It is a real marriage. I just want it to last longer than graduation."

"I... I don't know. I'm sorry, Peter. I never seriously thought about moving somewhere else. My whole life is in Savannah."

"I know. But lives can change. *Your* life can change." His hand was shaking slightly, but it was from the intensity of his emotions rather than anxiety. She was caving. He was sure she was caving. He wasn't wrong about her. She did love him. She wanted to stay with him. "We can build a new life together."

"Grandmama still needs me, Peter. You know she does. I can't just walk away from her, just because we get this wild idea."

"It's not a wild idea. It's what I want. And I think it's what you want too. You can't tell me you don't love me, Kelly. I won't believe it."

"Yes, I love you, but there are other things I love too. And I'm not going to turn my back on everything else. I'm just not."

"I'm not asking you to turn your back on your grandmother or anything about your life. I'd never ask you to do that. But if you really love me—"

She jerked away from his touch, like he'd burned her. "So now you're asking me to choose between you and everything else?"

He groaned, his excitement and emotional momentum starting to get strained with a slight edge of fear. "I'm not asking you to choose. I'm just saying there must be some way to work it out. Choosing a life with me, here in Eden Manor, wouldn't mean rejecting everything else."

She swallowed hard. "That's what it feels like to me."

"That's because you're using your grandmother and all of that as an excuse. You're afraid, and you're turning it into an excuse."

Her eyes flashed with anger. "You have no idea what I'm thinking. You think you can just read my mind and automatically know what's best for me."

"Kelly, don't be—"

"Don't be what? Don't be Kelly? Don't be a Beaufort? Don't be who I've always been? Is that what you're asking?"

He started to reply but her expression changed suddenly. "Sorry." She rubbed at her face and took a deep breath. "I'm sorry, Peter. I didn't mean to snap at you. I'm just... I'm just surprised and upset."

He sighed in relief at her more composed tone. "I know you are. I didn't think you'd be so surprised." He cleared his throat. "I've been crazy about you for a long time."

She shot him a quick look. "How long?"

He gave a half shrug. "I don't know. Years."

"So you went into this marriage thinking... hoping..."

"Hoping it would last. Yeah."

Instead of the softening he'd been hoping for, her shoulders stiffened. "Why didn't you tell me?"

"I don't know. I knew you weren't in the same place, so I didn't want to move too fast."

"So all this time you've been thinking... waiting... trying to make me fall for you?"

He was beginning to feel defensive, like he'd done something to be ashamed of. "What's wrong with that?"

She swallowed hard and looked away. "Nothing. Just that you've been trying to do this marriage on your own, the way you always have."

"I have not! I just told you I wanted us to do this together!"

"On your terms. In your plans." She shook her head. "I'm sorry, Peter. You've always been my friend, and I love you. But I don't think I can leave my whole life in Savannah for this."

He started to reply but then snapped his mouth shut, suddenly realizing that nothing he said would make a difference.

He'd assumed that her resistance would be easily overcome, but he'd been wrong about that.

Maybe she loved him, but she didn't love him enough. She didn't love him the way he loved her.

He should have waited a few more weeks, but he'd already tipped his hand, and there was no going back now.

He was still going to move forward with Eden Manor. It had been his dream for too long to turn back now.

He would just be doing it alone.

"Peter, I'm sorry," Kelly began, her voice cracking. "I didn't mean—"

"It's fine," he said, turning on the engine, his eyes focused in front of him. "I'm sorry I put you on the spot. You can think about it, and we'll talk later."

"Okay. I didn't mean to hurt you. That's the last thing I wanted to do."

He knew that was true too, and it made the whole thing hurt even more.

# ELEVEN

They drove back in silence—that heavy, aching silence that unmistakably spoke louder than words.

Kelly held herself very still, managing not to cry, although Peter's frozen presence beside her was like a wound in her chest, in her heart.

They were staying at a B&B about ten minutes away. It was a no-frills place, chosen for the night only because it was the accommodation closest to Eden Manor. Kelly couldn't believe she would have to spend the night with Peter, alone in a small room, after what had just happened between them.

She couldn't believe she'd thought this marriage would ever go as they planned.

Evidently he'd wanted more out of it from the very beginning, and he'd never shared that with her. The knowledge that he loved her that way—that he'd loved her that way for a long time—was thrilling and overwhelming and absolutely terrifying.

It was all too much to process, so she focused on maintaining her emotional control, minute after minute until they finally reached the B&B.

When he put the car into park, Peter turned in this seat as if he were going to say something.

She waited, barely breathing, desperately hoping that whatever he said would miraculously fix things.

Then he gave his head a little shake and looked down to unbuckle his seatbelt.

Kelly released her pent breath.

The next hour was spent in niceties, as they greeted their host and hostess, were shown to their room, and listened to a well-practiced spiel about local sites, restaurants, and shopping.

When they were finally alone, the door of their room closed behind them, Kelly's legs couldn't seem to hold her up. It wasn't even four in the afternoon yet, but she was utterly exhausted. She collapsed onto the bed—which was old but not an antique.

Peter stood and watched her for a minute, his eyes deep and speaking.

"Peter, don't," Kelly managed to say.

"Don't what?"

"Look at me that way."

"What way?"

"Like I broke you or something." She paused, emotion strangling her for a moment. "This whole thing isn't my fault."

"I know it's not your fault." For some reason her words seemed to have provoked him into urgency. He strode over to sit on the bed beside her. "It's my fault. It's all my fault."

"No, it's not."

"Yes, it is." He reached out to take her hand. "You were right before. I was trying to manage this marriage all on my own. I should have told you the truth before. I should have told you from the very beginning."

She shook her head. His words were earnest, honest, Peter-like, but they didn't make her feel better. "The whole thing was because of me—because I got so stupidly drunk that night." She pulled her hand out of his. "But that doesn't change the fact that things are still a mess between us, and they'll probably never get put back together."

She'd been staring up at him from where her head rested on a pillow, but now he stretched out beside her. There wasn't much room between her body and the edge of the bed, so he ended up very close to her, turned toward her on his side. "I don't believe that."

She tried to turn away from him since his face so close to hers was sending her heart, her senses, into a tailspin. But she couldn't make herself pull away. "I do."

He reached out to stroke her cheek, very gently. "I know you do."

"You said... you said that we would stay friends, no matter what."

"I remember."

"I don't know how we can still do that now."

"We'll just make sure we do."

"It's not that easy. You want... want more."

He wrapped an arm around her, sliding his hand slowly down her back. "And what do you want?"

"I don't know."

"So it's okay."

"It's not okay. I really hurt you before. You can't tell me I didn't."

"I'm fine, Kelly. I'm not going to let you go, no matter what. You're not going to lose me."

"I feel like I already have."

He leaned forward until his lips were just a breath away from hers. "Well, you haven't."

It was exactly what she wanted to hear. And his warm, strong, familiar body was exactly what she wanted to feel. Her mind exploded in need and relief as he pulled her head toward him enough to kiss her.

The kiss wasn't hard or deep or urgent. It was so soft, so tender, just the lightest brush of his lips against hers. It felt so good she moaned softly at the back of her throat.

"You're not going to lose me, baby," he murmured, his lips sliding over her cheek. "I promise."

She gasped in pleasure at the words, the touch, and wrapped both of her arms around him.

They kissed for a long time, nothing more than the brushing of lips, the light flickering of tongues. And emotion grew stronger and deeper in her chest, her throat, her eyes, until she felt too full, achingly full, as if one more feeling would cause it all to spill over.

She was so overcome that she was hardly conscious of Peter turning her over onto her back, slowly taking off her clothes, starting to kiss his way down her body. Before she knew what was happening, he was nuzzling between her legs, and she was clutching at his hair as he brought her to climax with his lips and tongue.

She shuddered through the waves of sensation and was surprised to realize that tears were streaming from her eyes.

Peter moved back up her body until his weight was pressed down onto hers. He kissed away her tears. "I'm still your friend, Kelly. Even if everything else changes, that won't. I just want to be your husband too."

She couldn't help but love the sound of those words, the idea of Peter as her husband—not just an accidental fluke but a reality for the rest of her life. She held on to him tightly as he kissed her mouth with more urgency than before.

His body was tight now with arousal. She could feel the bulge in the front of his pants, rubbing against her hip. With the sudden need to feel him all the way, she started to fumble at the button and zipper of his pants. He was still mostly clothed, but she couldn't wait to take off the rest of his clothes.

As soon as she felt his erection in her hands, she spread her thighs and tried to move him into position.

He was panting loudly, his body so tense it was almost shaking, as he used his hand to ease himself inside her. She was deeply aroused, wet and pliant, and she cried out as she felt him inside her.

He used his hands to lift her thighs so she would wrap her legs around him, and then he turned them over onto their sides. It was perfect, beautiful, trapped in the most intimate of embraces, touching everywhere, feeling him everywhere. And then he kissed her again.

He couldn't really thrust in this position, but he started to move his hips, and she matched his motion as best she could. There was nothing at all between them—nothing in the world—and she'd never experienced anything so powerful.

She was so high on emotions that she wasn't even aware of her body building up toward a climax, but it was— very slowly. Peter wasn't rushing, wasn't pushing them toward the end. All of his touches were tender, loving, making her feel safe. Protected. Adored.

Her orgasm surprised her since she hadn't been aware it was coming. She froze and then shook through the spasms, her cry of release lost in his mouth. As soon as she clamped down around him, he lost his control, and his climax took him just after hers.

They were still holding on to each other as their bodies relaxed, and he kept kissing her—very softly now.

"I love you, Kelly," he said at last. "And that's never going to change."

"I love you too," she admitted, knowing it was the truth. "But I'm really scared."

"I know you are." He released a long breath as he let her go. They hadn't used a condom, so she felt a gush of wetness between her legs as he pulled out. "But maybe you can think about it. I want you to be with me in Eden Manor, and I'm always going to want that. Maybe it wouldn't mean turning your back on everything else in your life."

His words reminded her of home—the old house, her grandmother, her sisters, the Kelly she'd always been—and with the images came a familiar spiral of deep fear. They'd been her security all her life, her identity. Without them she'd be throwing herself off a cliff, having no idea what was waiting at the end of the drop.

"I'll think about it," she said.

He relaxed, smiling as he kissed her one more time. "There's no rush. I'm not going anywhere."

But that wasn't true. In a few weeks he'd probably be moving up here, as long as the sale went through and Harrison Damon approved of the business plan and wanted to invest.

There was an end date fast approaching. The knowledge used to be a comfort, but now it terrified her even more.

Peter turned his head to look at the clock. "I've got to meet the first contractor in twenty minutes. I need to get going. Did you want to come with me?" He'd arranged to meet with three different contractors in the area this evening so he could put hard numbers into the business plan.

She'd been planning to be with him so she could hear the appraisals and ideas and give him her input. But she couldn't seem to move, much less make herself get up, get dressed, and get back into the car to think about renovations.

"I think I'll stay here if that's okay," she said, searching his face for any sign of disappointment. "I need to... to process everything."

"That's fine." He smiled at her. "Process all you want."

She smiled back at him, doing her best to hide the fear that was rising inside her. She must have been mostly successful since Peter looked relaxed, sated, almost happy as he pulled his clothes back together and slid on his shoes.

He leaned over the bed to kiss her again before he left.

When the door closed behind him, she hugged herself, wondering when she'd started trembling.

In Peter's arms she'd felt so good, so loved, so much more than she'd ever felt. But also so vulnerable, so naked.

She'd always known that losing Peter would be too much to take, but now she realized it would utterly break her. If she committed herself to him, fully the way he wanted, then he would become the center of her world, everything would rest in him.

Her world would be remade.

She sat up in bed, squeezing herself with her arms, so scared it made her dizzy. She needed to go home, to what she knew and had always loved, where things didn't change in such terrifying ways, where she knew exactly what to expect.

Without even making a decision, acting only on instinct, she scrambled out of the bed and pulled her clothes back on.

Then she found her phone, looked up a number, and called a taxi to take her home.

Peter would be a few hours with the contractors.

She'd be halfway home by the time he came back.

She couldn't let herself think about what he'd feel when he returned to an empty room. She would call him. She would explain.

But she'd always been a Beaufort, and she couldn't be anyone else.

~

"Wait a minute," Deanna said, leaning forward on the love seat near the fireplace. "Wait a minute, slow down. I know you're upset, but it sounds like you're being stupid."

Kelly had arrived home after nine in the evening. Grandmama was already upstairs in bed, but Rose was staying at the house that night so she'd still been up. She'd taken one look at Kelly and had immediately called Deanna to come over too since there was obviously a crisis.

Kelly had tried to explain to her sisters what had happened since she was too emotionally battered to hold anything back. She was really glad they were both here, but she didn't appreciate her sister's blunt assessment of her situation.

"I'm not being stupid," she said, taking off her glasses to rub at her eyes. She wasn't really crying. She was more numb than anything else now. "I really don't think I can do it. I can't live the life he wants me to live. I can't be the person he wants me to be."

"He wants you to be his wife," Rose said quietly. She'd always been milder than Deanna. "I don't think that's unreasonable."

"Of course it's not unreasonable. But it's not who I am. He wants me to live up north in Eden Manor. He wants me to leave Savannah and be an entirely different person. It's not who I *am*."

Deanna was frowning, clearly trying to understand. "I thought you'd always wanted to run a B&B or something like that. Isn't that what you always talked about?"

"Yes, but not in North Georgia. Not as Mrs. Blake. Not when it means I have to leave… everything."

Rose and Deanna were both silent for a minute, looking between each other and Kelly. Then finally Deanna's face cleared, as if she had come to an epiphany. "Oh my God, Kelly! You are just like Grandmama!"

Kelly gasped and stiffened her shoulders. "I am not!"

"Yes, you are," Deanna said almost laughing now. "You are so exactly like her. You're afraid of things changing. You want to stay safe in a familiar world that feels secure to you. Why do you think Grandmama surrounds herself with all these dusty old collections and refuses to give up the Pride? She doesn't want anything to change. And that's exactly what you're doing too."

"I am not," Kelly said, frowning. "It's totally different. I don't stuff my dead pets or anything. I just want to stay in Savannah and be who I've always been. What's wrong with that?"

"Nothing is wrong with it," Rose said, more gently than her sister. "It's totally understandable. And if it was what you really wanted, then we'd completely support you. But I don't think it's really what you want. I think you're using it as an excuse because you're afraid of doing what you really want. You want to be with Peter. You'll never convince me that you don't. You want to try something new, something risky, something that would stretch you in ways you're not normally stretched. But you're afraid. It's normal. I don't blame you. But it's not like you to let fear keep you from doing what you want."

"It's not just that. I'm happy here. I've been... I've always been happy. And I love Grandmama and both of you so much. I don't want to leave. What if it's... what if it's not as good?"

Deanna's expression changed. She wasn't laughing anymore. "You were so little when Mom and Dad died," she began, slightly hoarse.

"What?" Kelly blinked, not following the change in topic but affected emotionally just the same.

"You were little. You probably don't even remember them."

"Not much. Just... just flashes."

"I remember them. I was ten. I remember what it was like when our whole world fell apart, and we had to completely start again with Grandmama. Our new life was completely different, but we made it into something good. Even with all the strangeness, we've been happy."

Kelly nodded, her throat too tight to speak. Rose brushed a tear away.

"But things always change. And that usually means there's some loss. But you'll have something to replace it. You'll have Peter. And you'll have this brand new project to pour yourself into, doing what you've always wanted. That's what you really want to do, isn't it?"

Kelly nodded again. Of course Deanna was right. She was usually right about everything. "But Grandmama..."

Rose leaned forward. "You've taken care of her for years, and you've taken care of this house. We know she relies on you, but she wants the best for you, just like we do. We can figure something else out."

"She can't be alone."

"She won't be alone," Deanna said. "We can hire someone to stay with her."

"She'd hate to have a nurse or—"

"Not a nurse. We could hired someone to take care of things and call her a companion, like they did in the nineteenth

176

century. Grandmama would love that. I'm sure we could work it out."

"But that would be so expensive."

"Rose and I can cover it. It won't be any trouble at all. And you can contribute too, as soon as you and Peter start making a go of it." When Kelly started to object, Deanna went on, "Seriously, Kelly. You've done so much for her for so long. Far more than Rose and I have. It's our turn now. Let us do something for her... and for you."

Kelly couldn't believe she was actually crying. She had to wipe a few tears off her cheeks. "So I should really... really leave?"

She couldn't remember a time when she hadn't lived in this old house, surrounded by so many collected treasures from the Beauforts of the past. She loved them. All of them. She loved Savannah. And she loved her grandmother most of all.

"If that's what you want," Rose said. "If you want to stay married to Peter."

Kelly stared down at the ring on her finger. Peter's signet ring. Far too big for her finger. She turned it around so the Blake crest was showing.

There was nothing she wanted more than to be Peter's wife, even if it meant leaving other things she loved behind.

"What is going on here?" Grandmama demanded imperiously, after throwing open the door to the parlor.

All three of the sisters looked up in surprise.

"It is late. You should all be in bed." Their grandmother stepped into the room, her eyes pinning each of them in turn. Her gaze ended up on Kelly. "And I thought you had left me for that gadabout husband of yours."

"He's not a gadabout." Kelly wasn't even sure what a "gadabout" was, but it didn't sound flattering, and she didn't want Peter to be called it.

"Yes, he is. He's a bad influence on you, young lady. He causes you to forsake all of the Beaufort heritage. You would do well to be rid of him."

Kelly sucked in an indignant breath. "I'm not going to get rid of him. I love him. I'm not going to leave him. And you need to stop treating him that way."

Her grandmother narrowed her eyes. "Is that what you're telling me?"

"Yes, that's what I'm telling you. He's my husband, and he's going to stay that way. You're going to have to get used to it."

"And I suppose you're going to let him take you away from here, whisk you away from your home to some uncivilized region up north."

"It's not uncivilized. It's just North Georgia. And yes, I'm going to move. I'm going to move with him." Kelly realized what she'd just announced to her grandmother. She shouldn't have done it so bluntly. It was going to be hard for Grandmama. She should have tried to tell her more gently. "I'm sorry. I didn't mean to tell you like that. But yes, I'm going to move."

Grandmama tsked her tongue and looked from Kelly to Rose to Deanna. Then her eyes returned to Kelly. "I was starting to wonder if you'd ever come to your senses."

"What?" Kelly's eyes widened as she processed what her grandmother had said.

"I thought you would never come to your senses. It certainly took you long enough to make up your mind. You have always been the most stubborn of my granddaughters." Then, as if she hadn't dropped this bombshell, she turned to

Rose and Deanna. "I assume you two will arrange for a way for me to remain in our house. I will not leave."

"Of course you won't have to leave the house," Rose said. "We'll work everything out."

Kelly was still trying to keep up. "You mean... all this time... I thought you hated Peter."

"Nonsense. He's a Blake, isn't he?" Grandmama stepped over and lifted a hand to pat Kelly's cheek. "I know how to manage my granddaughters, and you needed more than a gentle nudge in the right direction."

# TWELVE

A half hour later Kelly was about to leave the house to return to Peter. Deanna had called the car service Mitchell used, and a driver had come to pick Kelly up.

But, as she was stepping out the door, a familiar car roared down the street, turning into the driveway, so quickly she was afraid it wouldn't stop before it hit the hired car.

When it jerked to a stop, a few inches before it tapped the other car, Peter jumped out and ran up the front walk toward her.

"Kelly!" His face was flushed and damp with perspiration, his expression urgent. "Kelly, I'm sorry."

She gave a little twitch. "You're sorry? I'm the one who left you."

"I know," he said hoarsely, taking both of her hands in his. "But I realized you were right. I was giving you a test or an ultimatum, and it just wasn't fair. You don't have to prove your love in any way. We don't have to move. If you want to be with me, we can stay here in Savannah forever. We can even live in this house. I don't care. I'll give up Eden Manor. I'll let it go without a second thought if it means I can stay with you, if it means we can stay married. I want you more than I want any of my other dreams. Just please tell me it's not too late."

She was so surprised she swayed on her feet. "You'll give up... Eden Manor?"

"Yes. Yes, of course. I'll live with you downstairs here for as long as you want. I'll give you anything you need. Just please tell me that it's not too late. That leaving tonight wasn't your final decision."

She was trying to make herself respond when Peter suddenly looked over her shoulder. Deanna and Rose were there, standing behind her because they'd been going to walk her out of the house. When she glanced back, Kelly saw that her grandmother was standing there too, still in her nightgown. All of them were right there, listening to Peter's urgent declaration.

His expression suddenly self-conscious, he looked behind him and saw that the driver was standing beside the car. He would have heard the whole thing too.

Peter cleared his throat, his eyes both ironic and amused as he muttered, "Maybe we should go somewhere a little more private."

Kelly almost giggled, emotion bubbling out of her now. It just couldn't be stopped. She reached a hand out to take Peter's. "Maybe the parlor?"

She turned around. Both Rose and Deanna were grinning now. They stepped aside immediately as Kelly came through with Peter.

Grandmama didn't move. She peered up at Kelly with cool aplomb and then turned to Peter. "Young man," she said. "In your attempt to earn favor with my granddaughter, please do not damage my parlor."

Peter blinked, and Kelly hurriedly pulled him down the hall by the hand when she heard her sisters giggling.

As soon as Kelly shut the parlor door behind them, Peter burst out, "Damage the parlor? What the hell does she think I'm going to do in here?"

Kelly leaned back against the door, laughing helplessly. "I have no idea."

"She's never going to like me."

"Oh, but she does. She finally told me earlier. She was just mean to you to push me in your direction. She said I was too stubborn and needed more than a nudge to get me to admit to myself that I was in love with you, and it was okay to leave her."

"What?" Peter looked astounded, his eyes moving between Kelly and the closed parlor door.

"It was all one of her devious tricks. She wanted us together after all."

"And there wasn't some nicer way to encourage you in that direction?"

Kelly was almost hugging herself with joy and fond amusement. "My grandmother doesn't do nice."

Peter ran his hand over his jaw, as if he were still having trouble processing. "So you... I mean, did your grandmother's devious trick work?"

"Of course it did. I'm pretty sure I didn't even need the shove. Of course I love you, Peter." She hugged herself even tighter when she saw the wash of deep emotion on his face. "I want to be with you. I was on my way back to you when you arrived. That's why the car was here."

"Oh, thank God," Peter muttered, taking two steps forward and pulling her into his arms. "Oh, thank God. I was dying the whole way here, thinking I'd forced you away. I meant it when I said I'd be happy to stay here. I love Savannah too. I don't need Eden Manor. We can live here for as long as you need."

She was filled with so much emotion that she was digging her fingers into his back. She couldn't pull away, so her voice was muffled against his shirt as she said, "I don't want to live here. I want Eden Manor too."

His body jerked slightly, and he pulled back enough to look down in her face. "You don't have to do that for me, Kelly. I know this is your home."

"It is my home. It's been my home. But I want a new home now—with you. I want Eden Manor. I'm doing it as much for me as for you. I promise, Peter."

He must have seen something in her face because he let out a rough, throaty sound and pulled her back into a tight hug.

They stayed that way for a long time, just holding each other. And Kelly couldn't possibly doubt the strength and sincerity of his love for her. She felt it in his grip, in his hoarse breathing, in his warm body.

"So you'll stay my wife?" Peter said at last, still holding her just as tightly.

"Yes. As long as you'll stay my husband."

"Not just for the forty-five days?"

"Forever."

For a moment he squeezed her so hard she could barely breathe. "Forever," he murmured.

Finally he released her but only to take her face in his hands. He thumbed away a stray tear as he said, his gaze holding hers intensely, "I'll make sure your new life is just as good as your old life. I promise."

She sniffed and smiled at him. "We'll make sure of it— together."

He nodded. "Together."

He kissed her then, passionately, eagerly, just a little sloppy. She didn't care. She felt exactly the same way.

When she finally remembered her family, who were probably still gathered in the hallway, waiting, she pushed him back gently. "We better save the rest of this until later."

Peter chuckled and gave her face one last stroke. "That's probably a good idea. I don't want to be accused of scandalous behavior. We should probably think about getting to bed soon. It's late, and we have a busy week."

"A busy week?"

"Well, we have to finish the business plan for Harrison and then, assuming he wants in, make the offer on Eden Manor. Not to mention the fact that finals start next week."

The reminder felt like a kick in the gut. "Ugh. Why did you remind me? Who wants to have finals at a time like this?"

"Not me. But that's the only way we'll ever graduate. After all this work, we don't want to blow it right at the end."

"That's for sure." She straightened her shoulders and smoothed her hair. "Can you grab my textbook over there? I actually have some homework I need to do for tomorrow morning."

Peter went to pick up the book she'd left on a small side table. A few pieces of paper started to slide out of it, so he tried to grab them in the hand he was holding the book.

It was a mistake.

The heavy textbook slid out of his hand and landed with a bang on the edge of the table. Since the antique table legs were thin and ornate, the table wobbled with the impact. Peter reached out to grab it but not quite quickly enough.

The table fell to the floor with a bang.

Kelly gasped in surprise, her hand flying up to cover her mouth.

One of the table legs had cracked from the fall.

"Shit," Peter breathed, staring down at the broken table. "She's going to think I did it while having my wicked way with you."

As Kelly's surprise faded, she burst into helpless laughter.

"It's not funny," Peter said, still looking vaguely horrified. "She's never going to forgive me."

"Yes, she will. You're a Blake. If she's mad, I'll tell her it's my fault."

"She'll know I'm lying. She seems to know everything."

"I know she does." Kelly went to help him pick up the table. She was still brimming with amusement as she told him, "You know, Deanna said that I was exactly like Grandmama."

"What?"

"She said I was exactly like Grandmama. I'll probably end up just like her."

If anything, Peter looked more horrified than ever, but even this grave prediction didn't scare him away.

Kelly figured that was a very good sign.

~

Three weeks later Peter closed the door of the downstairs bedroom in the old Beaufort house. He and Kelly were still living there until they closed on Eden Manor and could finally move north.

Peter couldn't wait.

Kelly had walked into the room just before him. She set her purse on the dresser and stared at herself in the mirror, as if she were still trying to come to grips with the way she looked now.

She looked gorgeous with her hair long, just the top part pulled back in a clip. She wore a cream-colored sundress and heels that put her head just at the level of his. Her dress had been covered by a graduation robe for most of the afternoon.

His shirt and trousers had been too.

"It's still you," he murmured, coming over to join her in front of the mirror. He liked the way they looked together. He wanted to see their reflections together in mirrors for the rest of their lives. "It's always been you."

She smiled and turned her head to brush a kiss against his jaw. "Thank you."

Figuring this was as good a time as any, he reached into his pocket and pulled out a ring.

She stared at it, and then she lifted her left hand to check out the ring she wore. The rings looked the same, both boasting the familiar Blake crest.

Without speaking, he slid the ring off her finger and slid the other ring on. It fit perfectly. He'd had it sized just for her.

"But I want to keep yours," Kelly said, her face changing as she stared down at the ring on her finger.

"That is mine. I switched it out for my dad's a few days ago so I could get mine resized without you knowing."

"Oh." She played with the ring on her finger as if checking out its fit. "It's going to feel strange without it falling off me."

"I don't want you to lose it." He cleared his throat, trying to read her expression. "Is it all right?"

"Yes." Her face broke for a minute, and she twined one arm around his neck. "It's perfect. Thank you."

He sighed in relief, finally letting himself kiss her. "You're a Blake now," he murmured. "A Blake and a Beaufort both."

"That sounds just about perfect to me."

It sounded perfect to him too, and he could hardly believe that he was allowed to relish the feeling, without worrying that soon it would be snatched away. She loved him. Exactly as he loved her. She was giving up her home for him and starting a new life. He'd never dreamed someone would do so much for him, with him.

That they could do it together.

When she pulled away, she was smiling, and she reached down to grab his left hand. "Now I need to get you a better ring since you'll be wearing it forever."

"I don't want a better ring." He touched the inexpensive band on his ring finger. "I want this one."

"But people will think I'm cheap, that I don't love you enough to get you a good wedding ring."

"This is a good wedding ring. This is the one you picked out for me."

"But I was drunk."

"I don't care. I'm not taking this one off."

She sighed, shaking her head at him fondly. "Fine. You're very sappy, you know."

"I'm only a little sappy," he corrected. "What's wrong with that?"

"Nothing. I love it. I wouldn't change it for the world."

"Good." Unable to hold himself back anymore, he kissed her again. And soon the kiss had become so intense that they'd stumbled over to the bed.

He pulled her down onto the bed with him, her body soft and willing. But she whispered in his ear, "We'll have to be very quiet. Grandmama is still around, you know."

~

Three weeks after that, Peter and Kelly were walking up the front steps of Eden Manor. Harrison had been impressed with the business plan, and things had moved very quickly after that. They'd closed on the house this afternoon, and now Kelly was unlocking the door.

Peter could see she was happy. She was brimming with it. He couldn't remember ever seeing her so happy before, and that recognition soothed the occasional tremor that wondered if she'd had to give up too much for him.

She'd given up something. Everyone did when they came together in marriage. But what they had now more than made up for it. Not just for her, but for him too.

Kelly put down the bag she was holding, dropping it on the wood floor of the front hall. "This place is kind of a mess, isn't it?" She stared up at curling wallpaper, at broken trim. It was obvious from her expression that she loved it, mess and all.

"It's going to take a lot of work."

"I'm excited. I love to fix things up."

"Me too." He released his hold of the rolling suitcase he'd brought in with him. "I guess we should start to unpack. I think that room downstairs is in the best shape, so we can stay there for the time being."

"Yeah. But first I need to get something."

Peter had no idea what she was talking about, so he stayed where he was as she ran outside. In just a minute she came back in with a box wrapped in silver paper.

"What is that?"

"It's a present from Grandmama. She said we needed to open it as soon as we got here. She said we needed to start our new life and home off right."

"Oh my. That sounds serious. What did she give us?" He was genuinely interested, and he leaned over to help as Kelly started to pull off the paper.

They got the paper off, and then they had to fight with the tape on the box lid. He finally pulled out his Swiss Army knife to cut through the thick layers of tape.

"Okay," Kelly said as she opened the lid of the box. "Let's see what it is."

She had to push aside mounds of tissue paper before she could pull out the object in the box. As she straightened up, holding it in her hands, both she and Peter stared at it dumbly.

It was a Siamese cat, stuffed to look lifelike, posed with one paw lifted in an imperious gesture, glass eyes disturbing and mesmerizing.

"It's one of the Pride," Peter said at last, as soon as he processed the gift. "Isn't it?"

"Yes," Kelly breathed. She was still staring as if she were paralyzed. "It's Igor. He was the very first one."

"She gave him to you?"

Kelly had started to breathe loudly, unevenly. Her face twisted as she kept staring at the cat. "I guess… I guess so."

"But she loves them. Aren't they her favorites of all her treasures?"

"Yes." Kelly's hands were shaking visibly.

Peter reached down into the box and found a lovely thick cream-colored card. On it was written in elegant script. "So you'll always have part of me with you."

Kelly burst into tears, so sudden and strong that Peter reached over to take the stuffed cat out of her hands. Before he could start to worry, though, her tears turned into laughter. "I can't believe she gave me one of her crazy cats."

Peter set down the cat and pulled his wife into his arms. "That's a gesture of love if there ever was one."

"I know. I know. I can't believe it." Her storm of emotion cleared quickly, and she gave Peter a quick kiss before she leaned down to pick up the cat. "Where should we put it?"

"We're going to have to hide that thing from the guests, you know. It would totally creep them out."

"I know. And some might be allergic, like poor Mitchell." She sniffed and smiled and gave the cat a little hug. "We can keep it in our bedroom."

"Oh, no. Uh-uh. It would be staring at me every time I try to have sex with you. It would be like your grandmother was right there in the room all the time. I'd never be able to get it up."

Kelly laughed. "Okay. We'll have to give it a place of honor though."

"Maybe far back in a closet. We'll pull it out whenever your grandmother comes to visit."

"It's not going in a closet. It's a Beaufort cat." She gave him a look of mock disapproval. "And Beauforts don't belong in a closet."

"No argument here. There's nothing in the world like a Beaufort." He gave her a kiss, his heart throbbing with how much he loved this woman and the reality that she was really his. "We'll find somewhere good to put it. As long as you don't have any crazy notions about beginning a Pride of your own."

# EPILOGUE

"Do you have any idea how gorgeous you look right now?" Peter asked, pressing Kelly back against a wall in the hallway of her grandmother's home.

Kelly snorted since at the moment she was wearing sweatpants, a tank top, and flip-flops. Her hair was in braids, she wore no makeup, and one of her bra straps was showing.

Peter's eyes had grown hot in a way she recognized very well. As ridiculous as it was, he must really think she looked gorgeous right now. He cupped her face with one hand. "Don't you believe me?"

"Not really. You said I looked gorgeous the other night, when I was dressed up pretty and we went out to dinner."

"You did look gorgeous then. You look gorgeous now. You look gorgeous all the time." He took off her glasses so he could kiss her without anything getting in the way.

"It's not even six in the morning," Kelly said, smiling when he pulled out of the kiss. "It's a little too early to be *that* kind of gorgeous."

His eyes warmed with laughter now, mingling with the heat from before. "It's never too early for gorgeousness."

Before he could kiss her again, a childish voice came from behind them. "Why are you kissing? We need to leave *now!*"

Kelly giggled as she pushed Peter away and smiled down at Jill and Julie, Rose's step-daughters, who had spent the night in the house. "We're done kissing now, but we have to wait for Grandmama before we leave."

"But our brother is waiting!" Julie said, frowning at her sister who was giving her silent disapproving looks, as if reminding her to behave herself.

"I know he is. As soon as Grandmama comes down, we'll go to see him."

Kelly and Peter had driven down yesterday, when Rose had gone into labor. The baby was two weeks late, and evidently the delivery had been long and hard. But the news had come at four that morning that the new baby was finally here, and they were all now going over to the hospital to see him for the first time.

"Oh, those flowers are so pretty," Kelly added, noticing that Jill, the older of the sisters, was carrying a rather motley bunch of blooms she must have picked from the garden out back.

"Yes, I thought we should bring flowers." Jill's eyes shifted earnestly from the bouquet to Kelly's face. "Isn't that right?"

Kelly grabbed her glasses back from Peter and put them on before she leaned over to kiss Jill's cheek. "That's exactly right."

Julie frowned as she peered up the stairs. "Is Grandmama *ever* going to come down?" she asked in a stage whisper.

"Grandmama is here." The small familiar figure of Kelly's grandmother was upright and meticulously dressed, even at such an early hour, as she descended the stairs. "The flowers are lovely, but what are you thinking, Kelly, going into public in such an outfit."

Kelly hid her bra strap under the strap of her tank top. "I spilled coffee on my T-shirt."

Grandmama tsked her tongue. "You should learn from your husband. He's always dressed appropriately."

192

Peter looked surprised and then adorably pleased as he glanced down at his gray T-shirt and beat-up trousers. As the two girls pulled them out of the house in their haste to go see their new brother, Peter whispered to Kelly, "That's the nicest thing she's ever said to me."

~

A couple of hours later, the entire family was gathered in one of the maternity suites in the hospital, taking turns gawking at the new baby.

Rose and James had named him Robert Beaufort Harwood. Robert had been their father's name, and everyone was pleased with the appellation, particularly Grandmama, who said it was a fine name for a fine child.

Rose looked exhausted and a little pale, but she was obviously happy, leaning against James, reaching to hold her son when Peter passed him back over to her.

Kelly wondered if she would feel that way, look that way, if she and Peter ever had a baby.

Maybe they would. One day.

After a brief lull in conversation, James asked, "So how are things going with Eden Manor? Rose said you're getting ready to start the work."

"Yes," Peter said with a seemingly casual expression that Kelly knew was disguising how excited and proud he was of their property. "The contractors are scheduled to start next week."

"Contractors?" Mitchell asked. He was the only one who hadn't held the baby, although Deanna had teased him about doing so. "You have more than one?"

Peter and Kelly exchanged amused and slightly guilty looks. "Uh, yeah," Peter said. "That's how it worked out."

"Why?"

"We couldn't decide," Kelly explained. "One was really good with the fine craftsmanship. I guess she's got connections to the best woodworkers in the area, and there is some historic restoration and stained glass that we want to make sure we preserve. But the other guy had much better prices for the basic stuff, so we decided to use both of them, splitting the work between them. There aren't that many good contractors in the area, and they both seemed fine with the arrangement."

"So one of the contractors is a woman?" Deanna asked. "That's great."

"Yeah. I liked her a lot." Kelly cleared her throat. "I, uh, found out later that she really doesn't like the contractor who's doing the other work. He seemed like a decent guy to me, but I guess they hate each other."

"Oh, my," Rose said, her eyes wide. She was still holding her new son, but she looked genuinely interested in this conversation, in her sister's life, a fact that caused affection to tighten in Kelly's chest.

"That should be interesting," Mitchell said with soft chuckle.

"I'm sure it will be fine," Peter said, putting an arm around Kelly. "They both seemed like professionals. It's not like they really have to work together. They just need to do their respective jobs."

"I can't wait to visit," Deanna said with a grin, "once the place is done."

"It's going to be a while," Kelly said. "But we're trying to get the work done as quickly as possible. We've got to get someone to do the landscaping and garden too. Then there's all the furniture and decorating. It's a huge project."

She met Peter's eyes then and knew he was as excited about the project as she was, no matter how big it was.

Just then, Robert Beaufort Harwood let out a loud, undignified burp. They all turned their attention back to the baby as Rose wiped a little spit-up from his face.

"He's beautiful," Deanna said with a fond smile.

Grandmama cleared her throat as she narrowed her eyes at her oldest granddaughter. "You could have a beautiful baby of your own, you know. I don't expect this fine boy to be my only great-grandchild."

Mitchell was visibly startled by this comment, but Deanna just laughed. "We're pretty happy as we are for the moment."

Grandmama just tsked her tongue and turned her gaze over to Peter and Kelly with an unmistakable expression.

"Not yet," Kelly said, trying not to grin at the way Peter had stiffened beside her. "One day, for sure, but not yet. We've got enough on our plates as it is."

"You are still very young," her grandmother said with unexpected gentleness. Then her face changed as she slanted a cool look back over to Mitchell. "But not all of my grandsons-in-law are so young. They should be moving forward with their manly duties."

Deanna giggled helplessly and gave her husband a little hug. Kelly was trying to hide a smile when Julie leaned over to whisper loudly in her father's ear, "What are manly duties, Daddy?"

Peter made a choking sound as he turned his face away, trying to disguise his amusement as he murmured to Kelly, "At least someone else is in the firing line of her disapproval for a while. I'll take what I can get."

Kelly had to bury her face in his shoulder as she laughed silently at his wry tone, at poor Mitchell's trapped expression, at the way her grandmother was always going to be the same.

Peter wrapped both of his arms around her, hugging her tightly for a moment, and Kelly came to the sudden, unexpected realization that some things had changed, but some things never would.

And it was good—so good—that her family had grown so much larger than it had been two years ago, when she and her sisters had been hammering down loose boards on the stairs and worrying about how Deanna could escape whatever suitor their grandmother was throwing in her direction.

They were still her family. They always would be. Even if she and Peter would be driving back to Eden Manor that afternoon.

"John Archibald Beaufort was a brave hero of the Great War," Grandmama said. "And he and his lovely wife had fourteen children. Have you heard his story before?"

Of course they'd heard his story. All of them had—even little Julie and Jill. But they all listened again to part of the familiar Beaufort history—made up of laughter and sacrifice and commitment and failure and honor.

And Kelly loved it. It was part of what had made her who she was.

Peter was another part. And she loved him too.

# ABOUT NOELLE ADAMS

Noelle handwrote her first romance novel in a spiral-bound notebook when she was twelve, and she hasn't stopped writing since. She has lived in eight different states and currently resides in Virginia, where she writes full time, reads any book she can get her hands on, and offers tribute to a very spoiled cocker spaniel.

She loves travel, art, history, and ice cream. After spending far too many years of her life in graduate school, she has decided to reorient her priorities and focus on writing contemporary romances. For more information, please check out her website: noelle-adams.com.

Books by Noelle Adams

*Eden Manor Series*
>One Week with her Rival
>One Week with her Stepbrother
>One Week with her Ex

*Beaufort Brides Series*
>Hired Bride
>Substitute Bride
>Accidental Bride

*One Night Novellas*

One Hot Night: Three Contemporary Romance Novellas

One Night with her Boss

One Night with her Roommate

One Night with the Best Man

*Willow Park Series*

Married for Christmas

A Baby for Easter

A Family for Christmas

Reconciled for Easter

Home for Christmas

*Heirs of Damon Series*

Seducing the Enemy

Playing the Playboy

Engaging the Boss

Stripping the Billionaire

*Standalones*

A Negotiated Marriage

Listed

Bittersweet

Missing

Revival

Holiday Heat

Salvation

Excavated

Overexposed
Road Tripping

*The Protectors Series (co-written with Samantha Chase)*
Duty Bound
Honor Bound
Forever Bound
Home Bound